The Life of

Marek Zaczek

Volume 3: The Precipice of Peace

David Trawinski

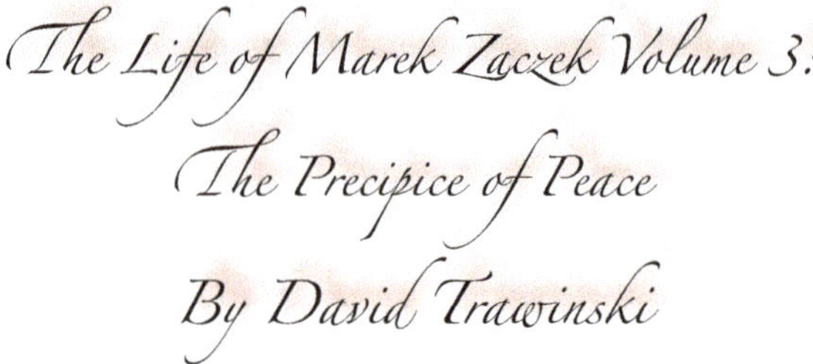

The Life of Marek Zaczek Volume 3:
The Precipice of Peace
By David Trawinski

<u>A Few Quick Notes from the Author Before You Begin...</u>

I have used an extensive number of quotes within this volume from published sources taken from several of the works listed in Appendix A: Source Material & Suggested Historical Reading. In order to differentiate these quotes from any given character's fictionalized dialogue, I have presented them in a center-justified, blue, bold, italicized font. Even in black and white editions, these quotes should readily stand out. I have also foot-noted them to the volumes listed in the appendix, and annotated them to the specific page numbers within those references where possible.

I have a habit of italicizing foreign terms as well, but these are not in bold. I suspect there will be no confusion for the reader.

One last bit of linguistics is worthy of noting here. The word *"Corps"* is used throughout this volume. It is a military term meaning a body (of soldiers) and is derived from the Latin word "Corpus" (body). It can be a confusing term because it is both singular and plural with the same spelling. For instance, one marshal's corps "was engaged," while several marshals' corps "were engaged" with the enemy. Also, while discussing Napoleonic Corps, I decided to depart from the military terminology of "Marshal Ney's VI Corps" to a more understandable "Marshal Ney's Sixth Corps" throughout this volume.

If you wish to follow the array of countries that made up the various coalitions that Napoleon faced off against during his many wars, I've included a guide in Appendix C *(Coalitions relative up through this volume)* & Appendix D (those that will play a role in future volumes).

Finally, if you are looking for a Polish pronunciation reference, please consult Appendices E (terms) & F (characters) at the end of this volume.

This novel is dedicated to the people of Ukraine who in their suffering under the assault of a greedy...

... and more powerful neighbor state, remind the world
of the need for a vigilant Coalition of the Just.

Figure 1: Europe of 1804-1807
(Current Borders Shown for Reference)

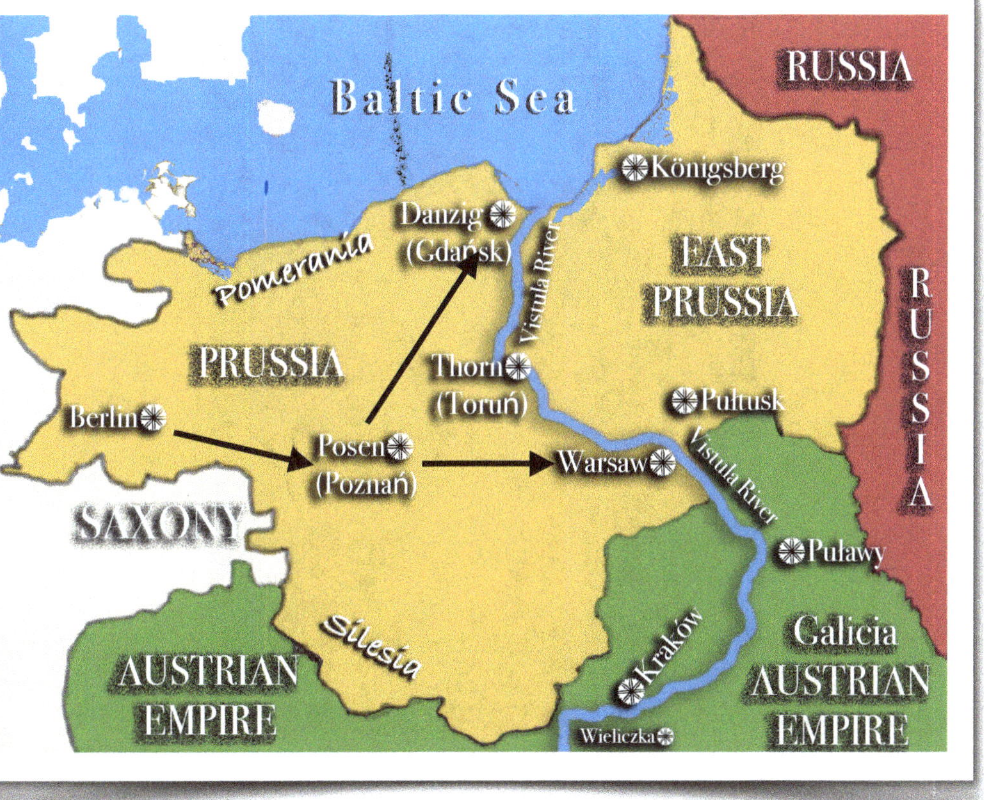

Figure 2: Napoleon's Prussian Campaign of
October 1806 through July 1807

Napoleon

"I will see whether the Poles are worthy of being a nation" [1]

---

[1] "Poland through the Ages," Monica Senkowska-Gluck,
Dictionaire Napoléon, Fayard, 1999

Talleyrand

Figure 4: Charles-Maurice de Talleyrand, French Statesman

"Poland is not worth the spilling of a single drop of French blood" [2]

---

[2] "Polish Soldiers During The Napoleonic Wars," Luca Stephano Cristini, Soldiershop Publishing, 2018, P. 5

Part One:

In Pursuit of Peace: The War of the Fourth Coalition Pushes Eastward

"All we can know is that we know nothing. And that's the height of human wisdom."

Leo Tolstoy,

War and Peace

Figure 5: A Polish Lancer of the First Regiment of
Napoleonic Polish Lancers (circa 1807)
By Édouard Detaille

Hunger is the fuel of ambition. Specifically, the hunger for acceptance, for recognition, and, ultimately, for total superiority. It drives an exceptional few men to seek dominance over all others. Their initial accomplishments sow seeds which sprout shoots, slowly at first, unnoticed until time erodes away the soiled facade of events to expose the tangled roots of their true intentions. Once firmly established, these clutch and grasp greedily at the goal of supremacy over all others, unrelenting even after the world has recognized too late the risk they pose and bands together in resistance. This is the breadth of our story.

Ambition can also be fueled by physical hunger; this is where our journey begins. In Warsaw, then as now, winter has a particular fierceness to its sting. Poles fear the drifts of snow that recall the ghosts of centuries past, or shroud new invasions of the Russians from the East, and the Prussians from the North amid its frigid, barren white mists. Yet, in January of 1807, Warsaw was comforted by the presence of its overwintering guests, the French Emperor Napoleon Bonaparte and his massive *Grande Armée*.

The shadow of Napoleon looms over the city, welcome as it casts the warmth of security, blanketing and insulating the once capital. The risk of invasion no longer hangs over Warsaw, for all along the Vistula River, stretching west to Toruń (the town the Prussians called Thorn) and north to Gdańsk (Danzig), are lined camps of the French marshals, with their massive throngs of battle-hardened soldiers. Warsaw believes itself to be safe.

La Grande Armée and its Emperor have recently defeated the Prussians at the twin battles of Jena and Auerstädt in October past. Within a fortnight thereafter, they overtook Berlin, driving King Friedrich Wilhelm III and his Queen Louise, along with the remnants of their army, to take refuge in East Prussia at Königsberg on the shores of the Baltic. Here, the Prussians intended to join the troops of their Russian allies, to await the spring thaw, and then resume war with Napoleon. Such is the overall situation as our story unfolds: the French in Warsaw and the Prussians at Königsberg, two hundred frozen miles to the north.

But where are the Russians? That was the overarching question of the day. After brief engagements with the French at Pułtusk and Gołymin, towns not far from Warsaw, the day after Christmas, 1806, the Tsar's forces were driven eastward and are believed to be overwintering near the town of Białystok along the Russian border. It was these troops under their newly appointed supreme commander, General Levin August von Bennigsen, that consumed the Emperor's thoughts, more so than the scattered remnants of the Prussian army. Poland's winter howl was fierce, and all were content to await spring's thaw. Or so it was thought.

The French Army was nearly eight hundred and fifty miles from Paris. Poland was a backward place to them. The roads were muddy rivers when not frozen solid. The temperatures plummeted too steeply. The January winds were too harsh, the women too chaste, and the food too scarce. With nearly the entirety of *La Grande Armée* encamped along the length of the Vistula, supplies to feed their bellies soon became exhausted. One French unit was soon pitted against another, marshal against marshal, soldier against fellow soldier, to capture food by any means necessary. Raids on each other's supply wagons ensued. The Polish peasants, their fields already stripped bare by an unforgiving winter's freeze, faced a dire uprising from the same starving, restless soldiers they had just welcomed so joyfully during the preceding few months.

An already weary army starved to intense hunger could become a dangerous commodity. No one feared the loss of control of these men more than the marshals of the French Empire under Napoleon. Among them, a single marshal dared to take decisive action. He planned to move his corps north in search of food, even though this act was against the Emperor's direct orders. That bold leader was none other than the impulsive Marshal Michel Ney.

Marek Zaczek was in Warsaw, having just returned from leave, spending Christmas with his family upon the Emperor's orders. He learned his battalion of Polish Lancers was to be expanded to a full regiment of four such units. Yet, control of that regiment would be awarded not to him, but to Colonel Wincenty Krasiński, an aristocrat's son a decade younger than himself.

Marek's life seemed to be self-imploding. He was losing his unit. By then, he had even lost his desire to be with his own wife and child due to the recent and cruel revelation of his own childhood's past, which had long been kept secret from him. He nearly lost the will to press on with the discipline of his soldiering lifestyle that he had come to rely upon so much.

Marek did not sleep well, but when he slept at all, he was tortured by horribly intense dreams. This January night, he spent encamped outside along the grounds of Warsaw's Royal Castle. Harsh winds howled out warnings from the waters of the Vistula, as if from Syrenka herself, that waterway's mythical mermaid and warrior protectress. Marek gave in to his body's intense exhaustion and his mind's crippling fatigue. He wished only to surrender himself to the peace and reverie of a calm slumber, and prayed it might overtake and displace his recent spell of vivid nightmares.

The wretched dreams started as they often did: with the frantic scratching and clawing of his two cousins, Andrzej and Bartek, flat on their bellies across the frozen lakes of Austerlitz. They tried to escape in that battle's final moments, their faces etched in mortal fear, unable to move on the thick, slick ice.

Then came the distant boom of a French cannon from high on an overlooking hillside. As can only occur in the torment of an embattled mind, even though his eyes were focused on the impending demise of his two cousins, Marek inherently *knew* the shot had been fired by the boys' father, his Uncle Jacek.

The cannonball whistled through the air, arching out a ballistic fate the two brothers could not escape. Marek tracked it over their heads, watching it grow larger and more ominous as it neared. So also grew the panic on the twin faces of his cousins. The round crashed down into the ice just behind their bodies, with the force of impact lifting the thick frozen sheet on which they lay upwards until it edged precariously toward the darkened night sky.

Those two Austrian soldiers, stretched out in their iconic white uniforms against the pale blue translucence of the ice, clutched its surface for a desperate grip, but the smooth emptiness of it was devoid of any feature on which to grasp. Marek's eyes followed as they slid slowly down then off the sheet into the icy blue waters of the lake. He watched them frantically try to swim as their uniforms soaked through until the weight pulled them under the surface. All the while in his mind, he felt the pathetic tragedy of dual questions: *Why did you return to the Austrian infantry after I risked my career to free you both from being French Prisoners of War? Why did you not go home to your mother, who had for years already blamed me for your being taken away from her?*

He tried to avert his view from this pathetic vision as his cousins sank into the lake water, but Marek's eyes could not be pulled away. They remained welded to the two soldiers, the weight of his gaze seeming to be the very anchor that pulled the pair under ever further. Marek's heart was attacked with a stabbing, gnawing guilt. The more his cousins thrashed in panic, the faster they sank into the frigid dark blue waters. The murkiness of the lake's depth soon swallowed and obscured them from his vision. Their flailing motions were hidden as the dark blue yielded to a mortuary gray.

Cannonball after cannonball continued to fracture the serene peace of the lake ice above. The bodies of his cousins soon reappeared, hanging lifelessly still, gently swaying in the water's depths, these slightest of movements resulting from the panicked thrashings of hundreds more drowning Austrian soldiers overhead.

As only happens in the realm of restless sleep, a mind not at peace with itself morphs from one macabre scene into another. The two lifeless but softly swaying gray bodies slowly transformed into a pair of gently dangling blackened boots of a single soldier. Yet, these were as dry as a bone. Marek feared their heavy stillness in his heart as his eyes climbed upward, even though he willed them not to. They dragged his subconscious self along. As they did, the wailing of the cannonballs' thunder transposed itself into the agitated neighing of nearby horses.

The view of the pair of suspended swinging boots slowly tracked upwards over the uniform of a Polish Lancer. The blue trousers striped in red along the length of the legs soon combined to form a matching blue *kurta* jacket with the red revers of its chest flapped open. The jacket's shoulders and collar gave way to a stretched but slack neck, hanging from only a taut rope wrapped around it. Then came the gray slab of an unflinching face. The dead man was none other than his Uncle Jacek, who, in his dream, Marek knew had unwittingly fired that deadly opening volley at his own sons. Marek's heart filled with despair, as it was he who had petitioned Napoleon to make a soldier of this gentle stable-master.

His uncle's corpse dangled before him, yet somehow the momentum of its undulations increased. Marek then felt the tugging of the motion upon himself, gently at first, but then more rapidly as it gained in urgency.

"Réveillez-vous, Capitaine Zaczek, se lever," he heard a voice calling in French. "Wake up, Captain Zaczek, get up."

Marek opened his eyes to the reality of his aide rousing him back to reality from his unwanted recurring nightmare.

"You have an order to report to Marshal Ney immediately in Neidenburg," the aide explained. "The Marshal is in dire need of a guide and an interpreter. You must leave at once."

Marek rose and stepped out into the frigid air of dawn. Light was breaking, but not as brilliantly as he had seen so many times out on campaign elsewhere. Instead, it humbly offered just a gradual transformation of the black night sky into the diffused gray of thick overcast clouds so common to the drabness of a Polish winter. He read through the order from Ney and commanded that his mount be readied. He looked forward to the diversion of this mission, as humble and unexciting as it appeared on the surface. He knew Marshal Ney well, and while this commander could be willful and often over-reactive, Marek had grown to like the man.

Late the next day in January 1807, Ney and Marek Zaczek rode side-by-side as the marshal led his soldiers northward in search of fresh farms to forage. They departed from their assigned area around the town of Neidenburg, east of Thorn, along the line between Warsaw and Allenstein. Ney's Sixth Corps had already been deployed the furthest northward, meaning it was the last corps for the supply convoys to reach. Many wagons arrived already raided, stripped nearly bare by the other marshals' troops, who plundered to address their own dire needs. As a result, the farms local to Neidenburg had been stripped clean of their stored fall harvest by Ney's troops. The only option left to Ney was to move his men northward in search of new towns and farms to raid, in direct defiance of Napoleon's orders to stay encamped there.

Ney's adjutants rode behind their *Maréchal* Ney, and *Capitaine* Zaczek, out of earshot of their conversation. Ney had been in need of an interpreter and guide, one he could trust as they marched deeper amongst the frozen lakes and marshes of these lands. He knew Zaczek was available and sent to Warsaw for him.

Capitaine Zaczek was happy to join Ney, whom he knew could be quite impetuous. Ney had dangerously demonstrated this on the battlefield at Jena when he charged his cavalry despite having received no order from the Emperor to do so. Ney's unit soon became encircled and was forced to form into a defensive *Carré d'infanterie,* or a battlefield square of infantry. The Prussian Dragoons buzzed around them and slowly killed off the square's outer defenders. At that rate of attrition, it would not have been long before Ney's forces were obliterated. *Capitaine* Zaczek and his Polish Lancers led the charge to rescue his unit.

"*Maréchal* Ney," Zaczek asked in French as they left the outskirts of Neidenburg, "do you not think the Emperor will object to your abandoning this encampment area where he has assigned your corps to bivouac?"

Marek had become very close to the willful marshal in the months since the Battle at Jena. As they conversed between themselves, he did not fear being so direct, as they were out of earshot of the rest of the officers. Otherwise, his query might be taken as insubordination.

"*Capitaine* Zaczek," Marshal Ney replied, "please forgive me for addressing you so, but I have not yet seen the order I understand is coming to promote you to Lieutenant Colonel, and to elevate your Polish Lancers from their current battalion status to become a full regiment. So, *Capitaine* Zaczek (Ney expelled the title from his mouth with a playfully belittling grinding of his jaw), please recall that I asked for you to join me as the eyes of a scout and tongue of an interpreter, but not necessarily as the voice of my conscience."

"Of course, Sir, my services are at your disposal," Marek responded. He was not, and never had been, a member of Ney's Sixth Corps, as his highly prized Polish Lancer battalion was assigned directly to the Emperor's Imperial Guard. Still, he had responded eagerly to Ney's request for assistance. Especially as, in his head, he heard the words of the Grand Marshal of the Palace, Napoleon's closest aide, General Géraud Duroc, as when they had so recently shared a Christmas toast. Over and over again, that most bittersweet news from Duroc haunted him:

'Your Polish Lancers are to be soon elevated by the Emperor from their current battalion status to full regimental status, effectively quadrupling its size,' which brought Marek great joy until the other boot dropped. *'The unit will be placed under the command of a Polish Colonel, Count Wincenty Krasiński. You shall be promoted to serve as that Count's trusted Lieutenant Colonel.'*

Thus, Marek would go from leading the lancers to merely being among those who would follow Count Krasiński's orders. This wounded him deeply as Krasiński was a decade younger and less experienced in battle than he was. Still, the count was an aristocrat, and as such, his selection would carry weight with the elders of Poland. Napoleon wished to continue to have their support, after all, it was their sons and their purse strings the Emperor wished to lay claim to. So, Napoleon would honor the bloom of their offspring with this command. It's sting still penetrated Marek, but he set aside these recollections and returned his attention to Marshal Ney.

"Mon Maréchal…" Marek began tentatively as he wished to communicate a concern he had formulated.

"…Yes, I know what you will say, Zaczek," Ney cut him off, "that you saved not only my unit but my own life at Jena and, by this brave deed, you feel entitled to question my decisions in the field. Well, my Polish cavalier extraordinaire, while I am still most appreciative of your timing then, not so your interruption now."

Marek was embarrassed that Ney would raise his heroics at Jena. The marshal was saved from imminent decapitation during that battle. For had Marek not called out in French for him to drop, the swing of the Russian's blade would have severed Ney's head.

"No, *mon Maréchal*," Zaczek replied, again ceding to Ney's great superiority of rank. "I only wish to make you understand that…"

"What, then?" Ney snapped at him. "That by being a favorite of the Emperor, the leader of his beloved lancers, you fear risking the Sire's favor being lifted from you by assisting me in what he may view as an act of insubordination?"

"No, Sir," Marek tried to reply, "I would never dare be so bold as to put my career ahead of the needs of your corps."

"Then, what is it?" Ney abraded him. "Speak now and directly, *Capitaine* Zaczek, as there remains much to be done!"

"Sir," Marek paused and awaited another interruption, but doing so only produced an impatient gaze from the marshal that pierced him as if he had been hoisted upon his own lance. "Sir, I merely wanted to assure you that by heading north into East Prussia, we may encounter the enemy. Might I suggest we head south, where that is much less likely to occur?"

Ney looked at Marek, whom he had, ever since Jena, come to greatly appreciate. This brave Pole rode like the wind and led his men in battle nearly as heroically as he, Ney, did himself. Most of all, Zaczek was fearless in the throes of conflict, as was he.

"You think I, as a *Maréchal* of the *Grande Armée,* am not aware of either this land's geography or of the movements of the enemy upon that terrain, *eh?* You take me for some kind of fool? The other marshals are assigned to areas along the length of the Vistula between Thorn and Warsaw by Napoleon himself, no? Please answer me, Zaczek. I need to hear your answer."

Ney's tone was playfully baiting, mimicking a superior being questioned by an officer many ranks below his own. Yet Marek knew the marshal was just having a lark.

"Yes, *mon Maréchal*," Marek finally conceded, "The *Grande Armée* is stretched out all along the Vistula's banks."

"And does that river not unravel like a snake down from the Baltic Sea near Danzig south to Thorn, then west to Warsaw, where it turns south again? So why in search of forage would I travel south, inside that tight coil of the snake, scaled with one marshal's corps after the other, where all food has already been devoured? The farms there are already stripped bare by this point. No, we will head north, as you note, deeper into Prussia. The German farmers are more prosperous than the Poles anyway, and more efficient by far. There will be much to plunder, *no, eh,* I mean forage. That look upon your face, Zaczek! What is it?"

Marek had reacted to the marshal's inadvertent slip of the word "plunder." This produced the change in his countenance that Ney had detected. Marek wondered if the plundering of Prussian booty had played into Ney's calculation much more than the necessity of finding food for his corps. Marek realized he had to respond somehow to the marshal, so he took recourse in honestly relaying exactly what was on his mind.

"Sir," Marek began, "I am only concerned with engaging the enemy. Surely, they will have troops deployed as we near their East Prussian cities."

"So why should that concern me?" the marshal blasted back at his Polish officer. "We are heading north toward Allenstein, Zaczek. We have 15,000 soldiers in the Sixth Corps. The Russian army under Bennigsen remains camped far to the east at Białystok. So let us engage a few pickets of their allies, the Prussians. Should that come to pass, all the better, I say, that we should overtake them, and bring yet more glory to the Sixth Corps."

"Do you not fear this will draw out a larger conflagration, Sir?" Marek dared to speak his mind, again afforded that luxury only by being out of earshot of the other officers.

"Marek," Ney said, using a tense and strangulated form of Zaczek's Christian name for the first time, as a mother might when tiring of a child's insolence, "what larger conflagration is there to draw? There are perhaps only twenty thousand Prussian soldiers left in the field after we have so severely depleted their ranks. They must be scattered over all of East Prussia. If we come across any, we are sure to outnumber them."

The look on Marshal Ney's face became more irritated. Then, he continued, "I asked to have you join my unit on this movement because I respect your knowledge of the area and of its terrain and people. However, when it comes to engaging the Prussians, and for that matter, to handling the Emperor, allow me the freedom of decision that I have earned as *Maréchal* of the French Empire. I am due that much respect, yes?"

The marshal's tone assured he was no longer jesting - there was but one acceptable answer. Marek delayed for a moment before rendering it.

"Yes, certainly, of course," Marek agreed, having sensed his marshal was tiring of his playing the devil's advocate. He, at that point, could only remain silent and hope the marshal would not march them straight off into the thick of the devil's den.

Marshal Ney's Sixth Corps headed northward, stopping after about thirty miles to encamp. Already, food from local farms was being foraged to feed the hungry soldiers. The 15,000 soldiers spread out like water poured upon the impenetrable face of a rock. Wherever Marek turned, he found only more men of war, although even after such a tiring ride, all he wanted was to be alone for a few minutes with his thoughts. He looked at the lay of the land and noticed the meadow they had encamped upon rolled off to the east. At its lowest point, there was a thick line of linden trees. There would likely be a stream just beyond, he thought, and headed off for a walk in that direction. After reaching the woods, he followed his instincts down an incline and soon found the stream. Aside it, Marek knelt next to a small pool to wash his face.

As Marek peered into the eddied water, not unlike Narcissus of Greek mythology, he caught sight of his reflection upon this still pool. However, instead of falling in love with its likeness, he searched the features of his face for the effects of the many curses laid upon it.

First, there was the loss of direct command of his Polish Lancers, the least of his maledictions. He knew Colonel Krasiński was a reputable leader, selected by the Emperor, perhaps only to curry favor with the elite of Warsaw. Krasiński would surely bring in his own underlings, and Marek knew he would be pushed aside, retained in name only to humor the Emperor, who favored him.

Marek thought back to a few nights ago, before he left Warsaw to join Marshal Ney. He had spent time with his friend Rydek from Toruń, the celebrated jokester. Rydek was regaling in the practical joke he had played on his old companion, having earlier told Marek that his wife Maya had been nursing another man's child, suggesting, but not saying, that she had given birth to it. Most aggravating, the child was not even of another Polish man, he would find out during his Christmas visit, but of a Cossack. Marek had not seen Maya, up until that visit, for nearly two years.

Upon the demand of Napoleon himself, Marek left his unit and returned home to enjoy his Christmas leave. He found all Rydek had told him to be true. His anger for his old friend flared, as Rydek had left out the fact that the child was the infant born to Maya's cousin, Bohun, whose wife had died during its birth. That was when Rydek laughed ever so annoyingly at Marek. He enjoyed the complexity of his prank, for Rydek had known all along Maya was merely wet-nursing her Cossack cousin's infant child.

"I could only wish to have seen your face when you first saw her with that infant at her nipple," Rydek said, mocking him. "I would think that you almost died, for nothing scalds like the searing heat of the truth."

Marek's face had not reflected any humor. "It was not I, but the Cossack, Bohun, who almost died. I drew my sabre on him."

"You mean he was actually there, still?" Rydek asked, astonished.

"Yes," Marek said, "and you had insinuated to me that my Maya had just given birth to his child. That was not in the least bit amusing to me at that moment. Luckily, I resisted the impulse to run him through just before Maya explained to me that he was her cousin."

"Praise be to God!" Rydek said, his words salted with heavy relief. "Had you killed the bastard, it would have surely ruined the prank altogether."

"Much else was ruined over those few days and nights nonetheless," Marek said.

"What exactly do you mean?" Rydek asked.

"When I asked Maya how she could produce milk for his child," Marek explained, "she introduced me to my own son - Czesław. He is only a year and a half old - but you knew that, you bastard! You knew I had fathered a son and kept it from me."

"But, of course," Rydek quipped, "to have told you would have given away my very elaborate subterfuge, would it not? I thought you would have been excited to hear from your wife herself that you were a father. A real father. Not just the fictional father to Maya's older boy, Władek, but a true son of your own."

"Yes, yes, I was," Marek explained, "until my Aunt Ewelina returned from Kraków."

"And this was painful in what way?" Rydek quizzed him.

"She returned after having identified the bodies of her twin sons, my cousins, who had died in the lakes at Austerlitz."

"No!" Rydek said, his voice heavily laden with concern. "The two you released from being prisoners of war after Ulm?"

"Exactly," Marek confirmed, "and even worse, my Uncle Jacek, their father, couldn't take the strain to think he, himself, had fired his own cannon on his two retreating twins. He took to the carriage house and hung himself in remorse."

"Nie prawda!" Rydek was shocked. "What a catastrophe!"

"You don't even realize exactly how much so it is," Marek said sourly. "*Ciocia* Ewelina accused me of being responsible for the death of the three of them. In her anger, she lashed out and told me the dark secret that my own mother had kept hidden from me throughout my entire life - that my father was not the man I had always known as Bronislaw the miner. In truth, I was ashamed to learn that instead of being that good man's offspring, I am merely the illegitimate issue of Duke Cyprian Sdanowicz, who took my mother against her will! Go ahead, call me a bastard, it is fitting."

"No, this is all too much," Rydek said, but kept himself from adding out loud what was running through his mind - *you are spinning too complex a tale just to get even with me. It is beyond belief.* Then Rydek thought further and added, "Isn't the Duke Sdanowicz Maya's father?"

"He was," Marek added, "but thankfully he is long dead."

"…But that would make you and Maya…"

Marek finished Rydek's sentence, "Half-siblings, yes!"

"Maryja, Jezu and Josef," Rydek gasped.

"In one sense," Marek added, "your joke resulted in my entire life falling apart. I told my *matka* and Maya I am cutting myself off from them both altogether."

"You mean this?" Rydek asked, truly astonished. "How can this be? You love Maya so! You saved yourself for her ever since that night of the Emperor's coronation. How many nights have I had to chase those French and foreign women alone because you were so devoted to your beloved Maya? I can see this is no longer the case. So, my heartbroken friend, whatever will you do?"

Marek rolled his shoulders, as if he had given his future little thought, which of course was not true in any way.

"I suppose I will return to Paris after this campaign, should I be fortunate enough to avoid the sabres of the Russians," Marek said matter-of-factly. "I may return to the life of a libertine that I enjoyed there for so long until Maya came to Paris and conquered my heart. Now, with what has been made known to me, I must leave this corrupted life here to fester in the darkness of the past. I certainly cannot continue living a life pretending to be wed to my own half-sister. More than that, I steadfastly refuse to ever again lay my eyes upon my *matka,* who kept so much truth from me throughout the whole of my existence! Also, I will no longer tolerate the scorn and venom of my *Ciocia* Ewelina. Rydek, I mean it when I say that I can only hope your return to your family in Toruń will be full of so much less drama and much more joy."

"So you've heard, huh?" his surprised friend said. "I leave tomorrow morning to join Marshal Bernadotte's First Corps there. How did you come to know this?"

"I have my ways, my friend," Marek said coyly. "Enjoy your time in your hometown. You should be treated as a conquering hero there. Do not worry, as my miseries were seeded long before you ever gave thought to your prank. It was actually a well-constructed deception, but sorrowfully, it overlapped just a little too closely with the dreadful secret truth of reality."

Rydek waited for him to laugh, to say that none of it was true, and to tell him how gullible he had been. But those words never came. The heaviness of his friend's heart never lifted. Rydek knew then that his suffering was all too real.

Marek returned from his recollections of the past to his present escape at the creek's placid pool of reflection. Yet the few minutes he had stolen away to be by himself had in no way refreshed him. In fact, it had only removed all the distractions such that he could wallow in his own despair.

Marek's head hurt. The peaceful, gently rippling image of his face fluttered upon the water's surface, but did not reflect the depths of despondency behind its still youthful mask. At thirty-four years of age, he was no longer a boy and was even beyond the years to be considered a young man. His life, having recently only found purpose in returning to Maya, by then, was void of meaning; it was as false and flat as his reflection. How desperately he wished to plunge his head into and beneath its image to drown himself, as if only in that way might his sorrows cease to exist. Still, he knew that he could never take his own life by any means, for even as depressed as he was, the soldier's will to live remained all too strong in him. Facing death in armed conflict will hone that instinct more finely in a warrior, ultimately denying him this false escape.

It was then that Marek heard a great uproar coming from a cook's wagon in the clearing not far behind him. He could hear intermingled streams of French and Polish dialogue, all piqued with great emotion. As he came closer, he saw a poor peasant woman lying in the dirt before the cook, who was butchering and dressing pigs to be roasted and fed to the Corps' soldiers. She was crying, apparently after having been struck down by the cook. He stood over her, a butcher's knife threateningly held in his hand, screaming at her in French.

"Now get up and leave, old woman," the butchering cook taunted in French, "before I take this cleaver to cut out your innards like I am doing to these swine."

It was clear the woman did not understand a single word he spoke. Despite the physical threat of the cleaver that she surely understood, she drew herself to her knees and pleaded, tears cascading from her eyes. *"Proszę, Pan, Proszę,"* she begged in Polish. *"Please, Sir, Please."*

"Allow me to speak to this woman," Marek said, surprising the cook as he emerged from the copse of trees along the stream. Marek could see that the peasant woman was on the verge of sheer terror as the cook swung the cleaver menacingly from side to side. Despite this, she still pleaded with the man. Marek took this to understand that the poor peasant *pani* had no other recourse than to plead on behalf of her family. They were in the direst of need.

"Choose whatever words you like, *Capitaine,"* the cook replied, reading his rank from his uniform's insignia, "but realize that I don't plan to give her any of the meat from these swine. I don't care how poorly she is feeling or how large her starving family is. They should have eaten these animals while they had the chance. But they did not, and now these swine will fill the bellies of the Sixth Corps of *La Grande Armée.* No, not so much as a morsel of their meat will go to her. She can plead all she likes."

Marek spoke to the destitute peasant woman, and she explained her situation. Having concluded their discourse in Polish, Zaczek turned back to the cook and, in French, said, "Good news, my friend. This poor woman does not ask for any meat, only for the intestines of those slaughtered animals."

"Why could she possibly want those?" asked the cook.

"They are very valuable to her," Marek explained, "for her to rinse and clean to use as casings for making *kiełbasa,* that is, sausage, to feed her starving children."

The cook was perturbed that this *capitaine,* hitherto unknown to him, was injecting himself in a matter in which he should have no apparent interest. He decided not to accept the resolution the officer had suggested.

"Good luck to her," the arrogant Frenchman said in reply, "to make any sausage without any meat."

Marek looked sternly at the cook. *Why must he be so obstinate?* A slow anger simmered within him.

"That does not appear to be her concern," Marek answered. "Perhaps her man has killed a deer, or a few rabbits or even the meat of a few crows. In any case, she cannot make sausage without the intestines that you certainly intend only to discard. Allow her to retrieve them from the scrap heap, and all is settled."

The cook would not give in to this man and would not back down from his position. After all, the feeding of the troops was his duty, and this officer must not be allowed to interfere.

"Well, perhaps I'll just make some sausage myself using them," he said defiantly.

"No, you will not," Marek said, slowly drawing his sabre. The cook's eyes grew large as he did so, especially as Marek pressed its tip firmly against the obstinate man's protruding belly.

"I have given you a solution and you have very obstinately refused me," Marek said boldly. "By doing so, you have insulted me. Now, here is the new solution. *You* will retrieve and rinse clean every intestine taken from these sows that you have slaughtered, and *you* will present them with a smile to this woman. Or I will cut *you* open here and now and present her with your own guts. One way or another, she will have the intestines of a pig. I assure you, I am not wasting my time uttering these words as a barren threat to you. You will do exactly as I say. So go ahead, and I will stay here until you so pleasantly present them to this *pani*. Begin to prepare those innards this instant, or I shall prepare yours."

Saying these last words, Marek twisted his wrist such that the tip of his sabre's blade cut ever so slightly into the skin of the man's stomach. "I certainly hope you understand me, *Monsieur*?"

The cook dropped the butchering cleaver in the dirt and looked down at the small amount of rich crimson blood that trickled onto the soiled whites of his apron. A cold wave of terror came over him as all color drained from his face, leaving behind only a pallid mask of disbelief.

"D'accord, d'accord!" grumbled the cook, meaning *Alright, alright!* Marek watched as a relieved smile slowly grew on the peasant woman's face as she watched the Frenchman retrieve the intestines from the scrap heap. He rinsed them clean with water from a container and presented them to the woman.

She had an incredible look on her face. A brightness overcame her. *"Merci, merci,"* she uttered to the cook, likely all the French she knew. Then to Marek she said, *"Dziękuję, Pan, dziękuję bardzo.."* *Thank you, Sir, thank you very much.*

The peasant woman ran off with the intestines, clutching them tightly as if they were gold bullion. After she did, Marek turned to the cook and said, "Now then, my good man, don't you feel much better?"

The cook only looked down and ran his finger through the small bit of blood that had stained his apron. "I'll feel better only after I have reported this outrage, *capitaine*. How dare you humiliate a French soldier of the *Grande Armée* merely to please a peasant? The marshal himself will hear of this."

"Capital idea," Marek said with a snicker. "Be sure to spell my name correctly, Z - A - C - Z - E - K."

"You are *Capitaine* Zaczek? Of the Polish Lancers?" the cook asked incredulously. "The one who saved our Marshal Ney and our soldiers at Jena? You and your lancers are heroes to the Sixth Corps."

"Yes, I am he, the very one," Marek replied. "Be sure to include all that in your report of this incident."

"What? This?" exclaimed the cook. "It was no incident, just a misunderstanding due to the complexities of such different languages. But you, Sir, with your mastery of both tongues, have remedied that. May I be so bold as to ask why an officer like yourself would even bother to take the side of a wretch like that peasant woman?"

Marek had been pleased with the cook's change of heart. At least until the man again showed his ignorance as he spoke the word "wretch."

"Unlike most of the officers of the *Grande Armée,* I was raised by a 'wretch' like that," Marek said matter-of-factly, "as a poor peasant child. Many days I went hungry, *Monsieur*, and many days my mother had to beg for scraps from those around us who had so much more. Since then, my lot in life has improved dramatically, has it not? Yet, one never really forgets where one comes from, do we?"

Many days passed with Marek supporting Marshal Ney as they continued to lead the Sixth Corps north under a gray canopy of overcast skies. It was now the last week of January, and the snows had been constant, but not yet crippling. The closer they wandered toward the Baltic, the clouds thickened, becoming ominously dark and laden with the imposing threat of a very heavy release. Marek thought that they not only choke out the sun but also forewarn of a great misery still to come.

The column of French troops halted temporarily as Marek huddled with Marshal Ney over a hastily unfurled map, "*Mon Maréchal,* we have skirted well beyond the Prussian town of Allenstein, deep into East Prussia. We are actually here, nearer to Liebstadt. Is it not best to bivouac here, before we might come in contact with the enemy's scouts that likely surveil these lands? After all, we are now very deep into the Prussian territory."

The marshal looked at his Polish guide quite oddly. His troops had once more been fed and wanted only to rest after a long march. Ney knew he needed at least another three miles of progress from them. After all, it was not good practice to give in to the first signs of fatigue of an army corps. They must be reminded of the need to press through their pain and fight against their weariness. Yet, Marshal Ney knew that Zaczek remained anxious, as if his worries of inadvertent contact with the enemy had not yet been sated. He valued the thoughts of this Pole, but the marshal was not inclined to give in to every discretion of a mere *capitaine.*

"*Capitaine* Zaczek," Marshal Ney responded, "we have been in Prussian territory ever since the Emperor led us out of Berlin. One cannot capture a land if one fears engaging the enemy. Had he that concern, the Emperor would never have taken Posen, or Thorn or finally Warsaw. Afterwards, he would not have driven the Russians out at Pułtusk and Gołymin, north of there. Soon, all that will be left of Prussia for me to conquer will be the port cities of Danzig and Königsberg, themselves. If your country had any roads better than these damned streams of frozen mud, the war here might already be over. Instead, the Emperor has decided it best to wait for the thaw of spring. Only until that thaw comes do I have time to make my mark. Do you see my point?"

So, under the earlier pretext of foraging for food, which was the very necessity that had launched their movements, but had since been satisfied, Ney still sought only the opportunity to engage the enemy. He wished to position himself as deep into East Prussia as he could, such that when the thaw of spring inevitably came, his Sixth Corps would be best positioned to do so.

"Ah, Sir, I see your point precisely," Marek replied. Indeed, he did, for Marek was sure by then that Ney held this singular ulterior motive, to be the first to engage the Prussians and gain great favor with the Emperor. Marek then considered how he could best serve Ney's desires. "Please allow me to ride ahead to determine a location to establish a permanent camp. After all, *mon Maréchal*, I wish not to lead your men out onto a frozen marsh."

"Take two of my scouts with you," Marshal Ney answered and then called an adjutant to gather the scouts. "I would prefer not to be marched out onto one of your many frozen lakes in this area, either. Our enemy saw the folly of that at Austerlitz, no?"

Marek cringed at the mention of the lakes around Austerlitz. The dread of all the miseries of his family that he left Warsaw to evade came stabbing back at him.

Soon, Marek and the two scouts rode out ahead a few miles of the thronging mass of thousands of Sixth Corps soldiers. The three ascended the ridge of a hill, taking cover under a copse of linden trees. They were surprised by what they saw. Crossing the snowy plains before them from east to west was an undulating gray mass. Given it being so far in the distance, Marek at first mistook it for a canal, one completely unfamiliar to him, whose waters remained unfrozen despite the frigid temperatures. Was its apparent movement perhaps whipped up by the wind blowing far inland off the Baltic? One of the scouts took out his spyglass, extended its telescoping sections, and scanned the distant horizon.

"Mon Dieu!" Marek heard the scout exclaim.

"What is it?" he asked.

"Russes," the scout answered, his voice quavering with disbelief. *"C'est une armée de Russes"*

"An army of Russians? No, my comrade," Marek said, grabbing for the telescopic lens. "It would take forty thousand men to stretch that far across our view. Certainly, you are mistaken."

"Certainement pas! They are soldiers. Perhaps twice that number, I might estimate, *mon Capitaine,"* the scout replied. "There is no doubt that this is the bulk of the Russian army before us. We must return and warn Marshal Ney. The Sixth Corps will be headed directly into it. If we do not, they will be annihilated."

The scout still scoured the mass of soldiers through the spyglass, ignoring the outstretched arm of *Capitaine* Zaczek.

"Donne-moi la longue-vue," Marek snapped, demanding the spyglass. "It cannot be the Russians. After the battles of Pułtusk and Gołymin, they had retreated east, reportedly to Białystok near the Russian border. Why would they be here, so far from the safety of their winter quarters? No, if it is an army you see, it must be the Prussians. We are too far north in East Prussia for it to be Bennigsen's forces."

The scout slowly pulled the lens from his eye and angrily collapsed its telescoping segments as a musician might crush flat the lungs of a concertina at his song being interrupted. Insulted that his observation was questioned, he then slapped the spyglass hard into the palm of Zaczek, but immediately withdrew it again before the *capitaine* could close his hand around it. The scout then handed the spyglass not to Marek's grasp, but to the second scout on his other side, who took it to peer through after extending its telescoping lens. The second French scout nodded in agreement with his companion's observation.

"Monsieur," the first scout repeated to Marek, "I have served as a scout far long enough to distinguish between a Russian army and a Prussian army, even at this distance. The Russians are no longer in Białystok, I assure you. I do not believe there are enough Prussians left in these lands to even form an army of the size that stretches before us, Sir! I would estimate it to be well beyond sixty thousand men, at the least. But do not take only my word on the subject."

His companion then spoke. The second scout said dismissively, "I assess there to be a minimum of seventy thousand Russians, perhaps even more. I agree we need to report this to Marshal Ney immediately. It appears the Russians are in the process of carrying out a winter sneak attack against our Empire's forces. I am certain *Maréchal* Ney will wish to send couriers to the Emperor in Warsaw immediately."

"We will report nothing that I have not seen with my own eyes," Marek said defiantly. Upon his uttering this demand, the spyglass was finally surrendered to him. He held it to his eye and instantly made out the details of two columns of soldiers marching from east to west. Then, he swept the spyglass along the columns and made out the shape of the horse-drawn artillery. Cannons, and hundreds of them, drawn by caissons of the most distinctive Russian style.

"My God, Bennigsen is indeed conducting a flanking maneuver with the entire Russian army," Marek gasped. "They are executing a movement against the western-most flank of the Emperor's forces. Those are most certainly Russian cannons. Hundreds of them. They are sweeping westward, and my guess is that they will join up with the remaining scattered Prussian forces. They are undoubtedly gambling to find a weakly defended point on the Emperor's western Vistula flank to attack. If they succeed, they will cut off the supply lines of the entire *Grande Armée*."

Despite the stillness of the three riders, their hearts pounded with a fury soon matched only by the hooves of their mounts.

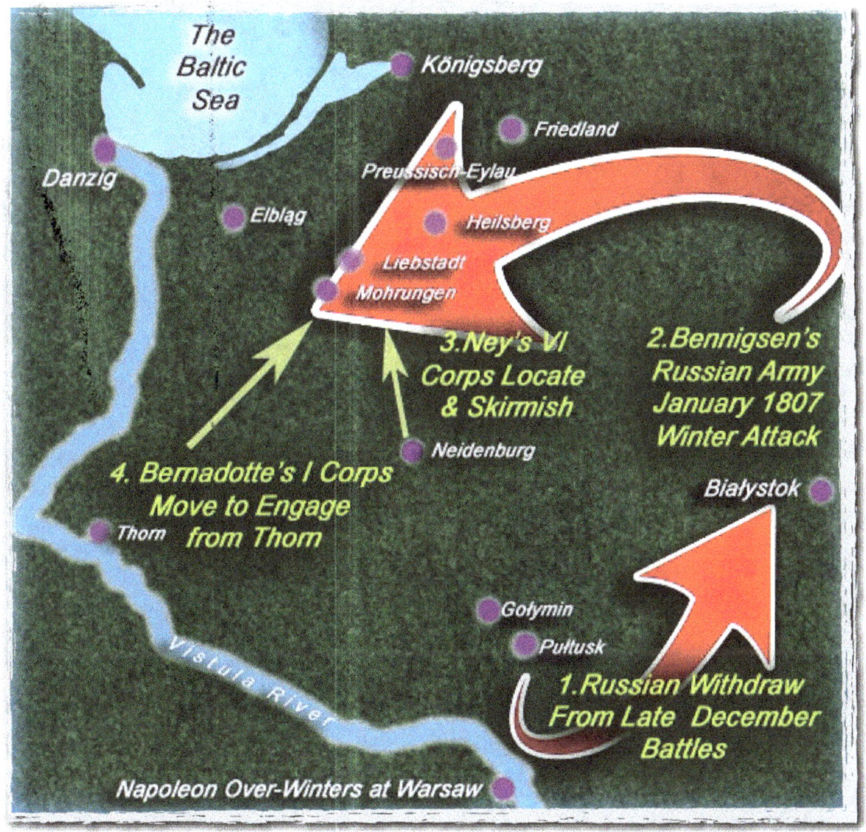

Figure 6: Russian Winter Attack Across East Prussia

Marek and the two scouts rejoined Marshal Ney and his still-resting Sixth Corps, well behind the ridgeline and out of view of the Russians. Marek briefed him, after which Ney spoke directly with his two scouts, who gave the same message. Only after that did Ney give the order to take him to the ridgeline so he could see the advancing enemy army himself.

Marek returned to the same copse of Linden trees with Marshal Ney and a small detachment of guards. Like Marek before him, the marshal refused to report any news as significant as this to the Emperor that he himself had not personally observed. As much as he trusted Zaczek and the testimony of his own two scouts, he had to see this tremendous mass of Russians with his own eyes.

"Bennigsen is counting on the fact that all the marshals of France will be focused in Warsaw only on gaining the Emperor's favors at the formal balls, and leading the parades and the cavalry exercises planned to impress our Polish hosts. He hopes to catch us unawares, cut off the supplies from Berlin and the West. Then he will surround and destroy *La Grande Armée* along the Vistula. What a very daring maneuver."

Marshal Ney said this all aloud as he thought it out. Marek was so grateful he had reached him in time to prevent the mass of his Sixth Corps from marching forward another few miles, where their number would surely have been spotted by the enemy and engaged. Ney's fifteen thousand troops would be no match for an army well over four times as large, with an equal advantage in rolling artillery stock.

"We must send notice to the Emperor at once," Marek argued. "You need to dispatch a rider as soon as possible."

"I have no one who knows the area well enough," Ney countered. "If they become lost, or captured by Cossacks, and the message does not reach the Emperor, all is lost. You will have to ride back to Warsaw, *Capitaine* Zaczek. You are the only man with whom I can trust such a vital message, but before you go, I need to dispatch riders to warn Marshal Bernadotte's First Corps. He is encamped along the Vistula above Thorn. He is the closest reinforcement, and he must move to intercept the Russians, even as you ride on to Warsaw. You must brief my riders on the route they should take to Thorn. After all, you know this land so well."

Returning to the French troops, Marek then stood over yet another unfurled map and directed the messengers on the best approach to reach Bernadotte's First Corps, warning them of the marshes and lakes that might not yet be completely frozen solid. Nothing was more dangerous to the riders than to wander out on thin ice that had been coated over with drifts of early winter snow. Their collapse into the freezing waters below would be disastrous.

Marek was given food and water to support his own ride of nearly one hundred miles back to Warsaw. He had been offered companion riders to protect him, but he knew if he was to make his way back in a day and a half or less, he would have to ride hard and fast. One rider was always faster than three, especially when they rode as swiftly as Marek could.

Marshal Ney saw his friend off. He reached into the pocket of his greatcoat and produced a small bottle of brandy. "For the night, *mon ami,* to keep you warm. *Bon chance!"*

Marek rode as swiftly as he possibly could, pushing his steed to its limits. He drove hard to the camp at Gołymin, where Marshal Soult's Fourth Corps was stationed.

Marek arrived well past sundown and rested at Gołymin for less than three hours overnight. He departed early on that second day. The fear of being intercepted by Cossacks was by then far behind him, and he rode with even wilder abandon. He made the Royal Castle in Warsaw at sunset on the second day.

"I am here to see the Emperor," he nearly screamed at the guardsman at the gate. "I carry an urgent message from Marshal Ney for the Emperor."

"The Emperor is taking no visitors. He is not to be disturbed," the guard said simply, relaying what he had been told.

"Listen to me," Marek said, "the enemy is moving to crush our troops at Thorn. The Emperor needs to be made aware."

"No, *Capitaine,*" the guard said stoically, "you will listen to me. As I just said, the Emperor is taking no visitors, absolutely no interruptions tonight. That has been made very clear to me."

"Then get me the Grand Marshal of the Palace," Marek said threateningly. "Get me General Duroc at once."

After several minutes, Duroc arrived at the gate.

"General Duroc," Marek began, "I have an urgent message from Marshal Ney. He has spotted the Russians in winter maneuvers near Liebstadt, not far from Allenstein. They plan to attack in great numbers against our flank on the Vistula near Thorn."

"Come with me, *Capitaine,*" Duroc said, casting an angry glance at the guardsman. "What is the matter with you, soldier? Do you not recognize *Capitaine* Zaczek? Did you not believe his need to press such an urgent matter? Perhaps I need to impress on your superiors their need for you to be taken from the Palace Guard and sent to fight the Russians directly? Perhaps then you'll learn to recognize the important information from the trivial? That is if you survive. Do I need to have you reassigned, you idiot?"

"No, Sir, General Duroc," the guard said, his head lowered.

"Sir, let him be," Marek interceded, "he had his orders."

"Perhaps you are right, Zaczek," Duroc said loudly so the Guard could hear, "if some of these imbeciles should be asked to think, they might become an even greater menace to us all."

Duroc then walked away at a furious stride. Marek kept pace briskly alongside him, even though Zaczek's legs were like rubber after his hard ride south from the Prussian-held territory.

As they strode throughout the Royal Castle, Marek explained in detail what he had seen the day before. "There was no confusion. It was the Russian army," he assured Duroc.

"You arrived at a terrible time," Duroc said, "the Emperor is entertaining a guest. He absolutely refuses to be interrupted."

"Who is this guest?" Marek queried innocently enough.

"I will only say it is his favorite among your countrymen," Duroc admitted, "or should I say countrywomen. We will have to take the wrath of his fury for interrupting him. But, of course, your information cannot be allowed to age any more than it already has."

Marek knew the identity of the guest immediately. Despite the Emperor's desires for their liaisons to remain secret, the truth had leaked from the castle. It seemed as if all of Warsaw was already aware of the sacrifice that the young, beautiful Countess Marie Walewska was being asked to make on behalf of her country. Despite her having mothered a son for her aged husband, Count Walewski, this pious woman was approached by nearly every influential and prominent Pole to give herself willingly to the Emperor, to satisfy his basest desires. For Napoleon had become infatuated with her, and their hope was that by having her lie down beside the Emperor in his bed, their country might rise once more to be restored to the ranks of the sovereign nations of Europe.

Figure 8: Countess Marie Walewska
Napoleon's Polish Mistress

Chapter 3:
The Trap is Laid

Soon, Marek and General Duroc reached the private quarters of the Emperor. The two sentries guarding it recognized General Duroc and moved apart slightly. The general's arm had only recently healed and was released from the sling that he had been forced to wear since his carriage had overturned on the roughshod Polish roads as it approached Warsaw. Given that, Marek could not tell if the tentative nature of his knock on the chamber's outer door was due to the weakness of his arm or to the faintness of his heart in disturbing the Emperor.

A muscular man in a white turban and colorful Turkish garb opened the outer door with a menacing glare. Marek knew him to be Roustam, the Emperor's trusted manservant captured in Egypt. The Mameluke was the last gatekeeper one must pass to see the Emperor, as Marek remembered from his visit to the Schönbrunn Palace in Vienna in the days just before the Battle of Austerlitz.

"I am sorry, General," Roustam said in his heavy accent, "the Emperor is engaged and will receive no visitor this evening."

Roustam's eyes locked on Marek, whose brow was full of sweat. He scoured the *capitaine* as if he might somehow present a threat to the Emperor. After a brief moment, he looked back at Duroc. It was then that Roustam remembered just how fondly Napoleon had favored *Capitaine* Zaczek over the years.

"I am hesitant to interrupt, Roustam," Duroc said, "but this is a truly urgent matter. *Capitaine* Zaczek has ridden for the better part of two days to get this information to the Emperor. Marshal Ney has uncovered a winter sneak attack by the Russians. A massive force is preparing to break through our lines at the Vistula and cut off our supplies from the west."

Roustam gave the general a look as if to say, *Can this be true?* The Mameluke opened the outer chamber door widely, inviting them both in. A fire crackled in the hearth, and in front of it was a dinner service for two, barely touched. Another door led to the Emperor's interior chamber, and Roustam walked over to it. Before knocking, he signaled the general and Marek to a section of the outer chamber where they were denied any sightlines into that interior room.

"WHAT? WHAT IS IT, ROUSTAM?" The Emperor's voice bellowed angrily from behind the massive door. *"DID I NOT INSTRUCT YOU THAT THERE WERE TO BE NO INTERRUPTIONS THIS EVENING?"*

"Sire, forgive me," the manservant explained, "but General Duroc is here with an urgent message regarding the Russians from Marshal Ney."

Then the three men in the outer chamber heard the Emperor exclaim, *"Ney! Always Ney! Merde!"* followed by a second of hesitant silence. Then, in a lower voice, they heard him say:

"C'est impossible! I finally have your lovely delightful company all to myself for a few exquisite hours only to have these damn Russians tear me away from you, my Countess. Forgive me, I promise you that I will not be away from you for long."

A minute later, Napoleon emerged from the interior chamber. He looked angrily at Duroc first, then appeared to be surprised that *Roustam* had even permitted Capitaine Zaczek to enter along with the general.

"So, it is you, Zaczek," Napoleon said, "I was disappointed to learn you had joined Ney in abandoning the area I assigned to him at Neidenburg. And to what end? To wander aimlessly through Prussia, only to be discovered and give the Russians reason to be outraged. Ney is an imbecile to disregard my orders so blatantly. He will pay the price. So, what is this news from that rascal Ney? Speak, Zaczek, your Emperor awaits!"

Marek was flustered. Speechless. Napoleon was outraged. His arms flailed as he spoke of Ney's disregard. His cheeks became flushed as all restraint drained from him. Noticing the mud on the Pole's boots and leggings, he added, "You come before your Emperor making so disgraceful a presentation of yourself?"

"Sire," Duroc decided to break the silence from Marek's loss of words, *"Capitaine* Zaczek has ridden for the better part of two days to assure Marshal Ney's urgent message reached your ears, and none other."

"General Duroc," Napoleon snapped, "will you allow Zaczek to speak this news already? Stop interrupting us. What good is his ride if his tongue fails him? *Eh?* So, Zaczek, what is this calamity with the Russians that is so important that I am to be disturbed from my rest? Go on, Zaczek…"

"Sire," Marek began hesitatingly, "Marshal Ney has instructed me to relay to you that the Russian General Bennigsen has an army of some seventy thousand troops and four hundred guns crossing Prussia near Liebstadt."

"So, Ney, the reckless idiot, has prompted this attack? His movements with the Sixth Corps have drawn the Russians forth from Białystok?"

"No, my Emperor," Marek reassured him, "Marshal Ney's forces were not spotted. He would like to engage Bennigsen, but only has the Sixth Corps…"

"Yes, of course, only fifteen thousand men…" Napoleon said, moving over to the map table - the same table that held the dinner, which was mostly untouched.

"Roustam," the Emperor barked, "clear away these plates and bring out the map of East Prussia." The Mameluke did so, taking away the dinner service without causing any clatter at all.

"Marshal Ney has alerted Marshal Bernadotte and his First Corps," Marek said, "while I rode here to Warsaw."

"So then, am I the last to learn of this invasion?" Napoleon waited impatiently for the map to be unfurled, his foot tapping in a rapid manner on the floor. Once it was laid before him, he placed his finger on the map at the location of Liebstadt. "Here, *eh?* When did this sighting occur, Zaczek?"

"Early yesterday, Sire."

"How is it you are here?" the Emperor asked. "That is a two-and-a-half-day ride."

"Not for me, Sire," Marek said. "Not given the importance of this message arriving for you, Sire."

"Then you have done well," the Emperor said. "Very well indeed. Have you seen this army? With your own eyes, yes?"

"Yes, Sire," Marek said, "it is at least seventy thousand strong, by my count, with some four hundred pieces of artillery. They mean to crash through our left flank along the Vistula."

"Then we must invite them to continue on in their folly, Zaczek. Duroc, get riders ready. They are to await my dispatch. I will need to send orders out to Marshals Ney, Bernadotte, Soult, and Davout. We have an opportunity to teach these Russians a lesson. They will learn that it is not only they who can fight in these winter conditions."

"What have you in mind, my Emperor?" Duroc asked.

"It appears General Bennigsen wishes to catch us resting unawares during winter quarters," Napoleon thought out loud. "He desires to attack our weak left flank along the Vistula River between Thorn and Danzig. So, we will have Marshal Bernadotte and his First Corps engage them and fight rear-guard actions as they retreat back toward Thorn. As Bennigsen follows them, I will drive northward with Soult's Fourth Corps, Davout's Third Corps, and Augereau's Seventh Corps to close in on them from behind. We will quietly reinforce Bernadotte at Thorn, of course, with troops amassed for the coming siege at Danzig under Marshal Lefebvre. Bennigsen's massive army will be crushed between our two pincers, but only if the Russians take the bait and follow Bernadotte all the way back to Thorn."

"Outstanding, Sire," Duroc said. "They will never suspect they are fighting their way directly into your trap."

"Ready the riders!" Napoleon commanded. "Assure they have relays so not an hour is wasted in getting my orders out to the field. Time is of the essence. We move out in the morning. I will prepare the wording of the order, so have the scribes ready to make copies as needed."

"Sire, it will be my great honor to courier your order to Marshal Ney," Marek said.

"No, Zaczek," Napoleon replied. "You have muddied your lancer's uniform enough as a mere courier. Tomorrow you will ride alongside me as my guide. You know the lay of the land, and I trust you most as an interpreter. I cannot afford for even a single unit to imperil itself by misreading a map. I want someone with me who has ridden the terrain."

A burst of pride swelled within Marek's chest. For even at Austerlitz, where he had pointed out the features of the terrain to the Emperor, he was not allowed to ride astride Napoleon. Tomorrow, that honor would be his.

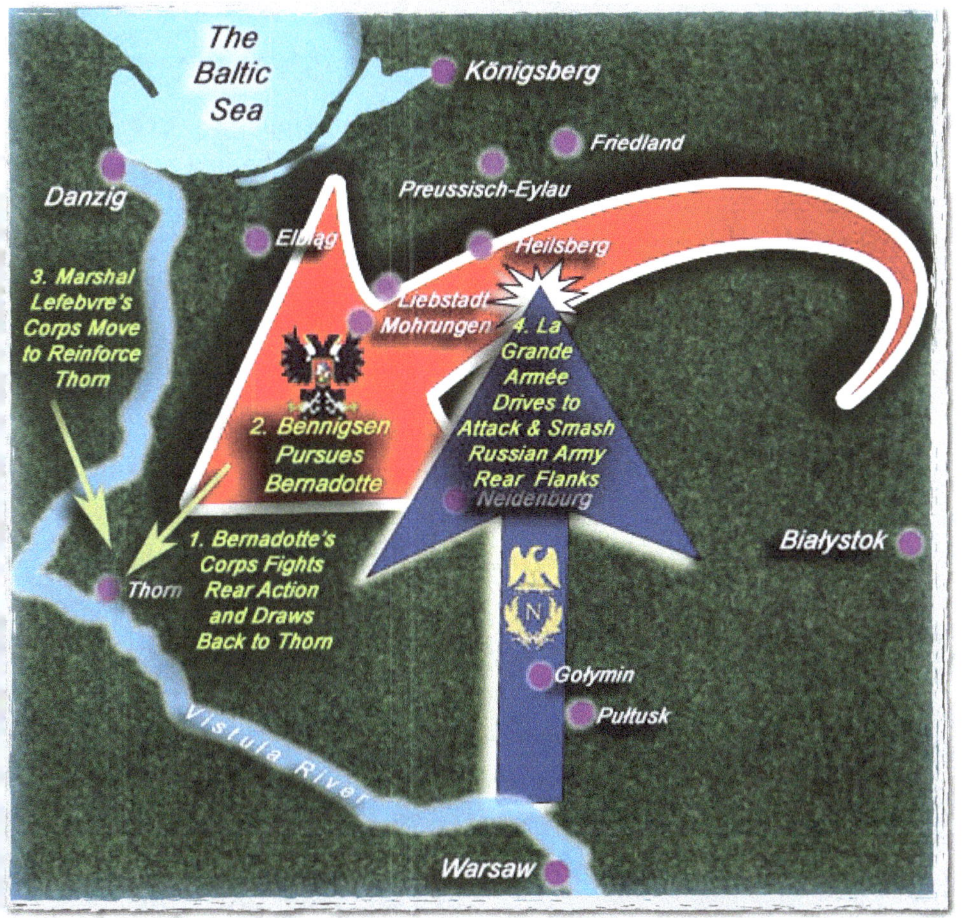

Figure 9: Napoleon's Russian Trap

"But, Sire," Marek felt it his duty to object, "certainly that honor should go to General Dąbrowski or Colonel Krasiński?"

"No, Zaczek," the Emperor was fuming again, "it is your honor, your reward for bringing this message so directly to me. I already have General Dąbrowski assisting Marshal Lefebvre in preparing the plans to besiege Danzig, and I have Colonel Krasiński evaluating the sons of Polish noblemen for the expansion of your beloved lancers. No, Zaczek, you will accompany me, with the Imperial Guard Cavalry, where you should have remained these past days instead of so defiantly attaching yourself to Marshal Ney and his Sixth Corps."

Marek dropped his head at the Emperor's scolding. Napoleon walked over to him, this Polish rider who had been with him since rescuing his beloved steed at the bridge at Lodi in Italy over a decade earlier. He reached down and with his forefinger lifted Marek's chin.

"But, of course," the Emperor said with a smile, "it appears we are quite fortunate that you did exactly that, are we not? Now, if only Ney can resist his desire to attack the Russians alone and spoil my trap for them!"

"I do not think he will, Sire," Marek added. "He is outnumbered four-to-one in infantry and even more so in artillery."

"Ah, Zaczek," Napoleon replied, "you have said the magic word, *'think.'* Marshal Ney does not always think before he acts. Was it not your lancers that Marshal Lannes had to risk at Jena to rescue him because Ney did not think before he charged his cavalry? Yes, of course it was you. Ney is very brave, indeed. Sometimes, a bit too much so, no?"

"Yes, Sire," Marek replied.

"I will assemble the messengers and the scribes, your Imperial Highness," General Duroc said as he moved to exit from the room. "I shall return momentarily to await your orders, Sire."

"Be gone, both of you," Napoleon said. "Zaczek, get some rest tonight. You will need your wits about you in the morning. If we are to spring this trap on General Bennigsen, we may need to quickly maneuver through these lands so full of marshes and lakes. I hope you know them as well as I think you do. It is hard to fight Russians when one's horse is bogged down in mud up to its fetlocks. Now, leave me, I have much to do."

"Yes, of course, Sire," Marek replied and headed to the door. "I know these lands well and will not fail you, my Emperor! Not so long as there remains a single breath in my lungs."

"Zaczek," Napoleon replied, "if there is no longer any breath in your lungs, it means by definition that you have not served me well. Go on and get some sleep now. You have certainly earned it."

With those words, the Emperor retreated to the interior room and closed the door behind them. As they exited, Duroc and Marek could hear him say to his guest, *"A thousand pardons, my dearest Marie. It appears your Polish homelands are threatened by a Russian invasion pressing through the winter snows. Give me a half hour to write out my orders, then afterwards, I will be all yours. In the morning, I must depart, so let us make the most of the few sweet remaining hours we have together."*

Chapter 4:
The Luck of the Cossacks

Cossacks for centuries had been warriors of shifting allegiances. Especially those of Zaporozhian descent, or of the "Zaporozhian Host," as are called those who come from beyond the River Dnieper. These masterful horseback combatants aligned and re-aligned themselves, off and on, with the Winged Hussars of the Polish-Lithuanian Commonwealth, the cavalry of the Russian Armies of the Tsar, and on occasion, even with the Muslim riders of the Crimean Turks. Yet, even when they fought with these organized militia, the Cossacks always resisted being incorporated directly into their ranks, preferring to remain separate as auxiliary roving bands of marauding warrior scouts.

The Cossacks came from the steppes of Eurasia, the large swaths of open lands known locally as *"The Sich."* Covering vast distances to fight the Poles, Russians, or Turks, not to mention the dreaded Tartar hordes, required that they become masters of the horse. Most could ride effortlessly for uninterrupted spans that stretch the imagination. They could live off the land or forage for food for weeks on end, if not months. They were a product of their terrain, the Ukraine, whose population alternately welcomed and then rejected both the Poles and the Russians over the centuries. Most famously, they rose up against their Polish overlords during the Polish-Cossack war of 1647-1648 when the *Hetman,* or military commander, named Bohdan Khmelnytsky, broke away from the Polish forces and declared a Cossack State in *the Sich.*

Figure 10: A Cossack of the Zaporozhian Host

In January 1807, bands of Cossacks had committed to align themselves with the Tsarist Armies moving westward to defend East Prussia against Napoleon's invading forces. One such group was led by a brave warrior who himself had been named after the famed Bohdan Khmelnytsky. He went by the single name, "Bohun," an earthier variant of the name Bohdan.

Bohun had just rejoined his band in the field near Białystok, after New Year's Day. In the late Autumn of 1806, he had departed from the unit of Cossacks he led to attend to his pregnant wife's delivery of their first son in Kiev. Tragically, Bohun's wife died during that child's birth, and his newborn infant son needed to be left in capable and nurturing hands before he could rejoin his band of Cossacks. So Bohun traveled with the child to Warsaw, such that he could leave the infant with his cousin Maya.

After having rested there through the Christmas and New Year's holidays, Bohun traveled to the Polish town of Białystok near the Russian border. The Russian army was then quartered there, after having recently withdrawn from the Battle of Pułtusk against Napoleon's forces. Upon his arrival, Bohun committed his band of a dozen Cossacks to the Tsar's Army, whereupon they were assigned an area to scout for any French forces moving north.

"I have always favored the Cossacks," General Bennigsen was known to have said, "for they are great warriors, but even more they tend to be a rather lucky band of marauders."

True to the comment of the newly appointed overall commander of the Tsar's forces, in mid-January, Bohun's Cossacks stumbled upon a French courier in the lands north of the Vistula and west of Warsaw at a small stream. Watering his horse, the rider had been observed examining and re-examining a map, trying to ascertain his exact position. He was obviously lost. Bohun assumed him to be a new recruit from France, unfamiliar with the countryside. When they converged on the rider, he mounted and attempted to outrun them.

The Cossacks found this to be nothing more than a delightful amusement and soon ran down the man before encircling him. As they did, they saw the rider unsuccessfully striking matches in an attempt to burn the message he was couriering. They subdued the courier and seized the orders he carried. As Bohun had thought, the rider spoke only French, and not a trace of Polish, and certainly not any of the tongues from further east - Russian or Ukrainian.

The message was hand-scripted in flowing French characters, and as such, it was as much a mystery to the Cossacks as if it had been encoded in Egyptian Hieroglyphs. The Cossacks had no common tongue with which to query the rider directly. Bohun spoke Ukrainian, Russian, and Polish, but not French. The rider spoke only French and a little German. The Cossacks debated killing him, but decided it was best to keep him alive to be interrogated by others.

"I have a cousin in Warsaw," Bohun said to his second in command, the Cossack Fadeyka, "she could interpret this for us."

"Sure, Bohun," he said, "we will just parade ourselves, a dozen Cossacks, weaving ourselves through the throngs of French soldiers quartered there."

"Don't be such a horse's ass," Bohun said. "For one, I doubt they have even received word yet that we Cossacks have aligned ourselves again with the Russian troops. But, in any case, I meant only for one of us to slip into that city in civilian clothes. I was just there visiting Maya, who speaks and reads French."

"No," Fadeyka said, "I do not think that is a good idea. We have no way to copy it, except character for character by hand. If you were caught with it, not only would we lose the message, but our leader as well. Besides, once it is in your cousin's head, she could relay it to others. It is your decision, Bohun, but I suggest we take it and the courier back to Białystok. The Russians surely have many among them who can read French."

"Yes, of course, you are right, Fadeyka," Bohun admitted. He wondered how much of his thought was tainted by his desire to see Maya, and his son, Orest, again, for whom she cared. "My only concern with going straight to the Russians is that if we have simply intercepted an order which may say nothing more interesting than to feed the cavalry horses half-rations until more supplies arrive, we will look like complete fools."

"And if it is some grand order," Fadeyka rebutted, "that puts the whole Russian army in great peril, and you get caught with it in Warsaw, we will look like traitors. Besides, why would this courier try to burn an order so benign as half-rations?"

"Yes, as usual, I think you are right, my friend," Bohun committed. "General Bennigsen has left Białystok for points unknown, but I believe the Russian General Buxhowden still is near Białystok with a reserve of the Tsar's forces. We will take this French rider to them. They will know what to do, and if we make fools of ourselves, at least it will not be in front of the Russian Supreme Commander."

Bohun had kept from Fadeyka that his cousin was married to a Polish cavalry officer in the service of the French. He feared it would somehow undermine his command. They traveled to Białystok and presented the captured order and the courier himself.

"It is as you thought," said the interrogator to Bohun. who had demanded to remain in the room as the messenger was queried. They spoke in Russian, the only tongue Bohun knew other than Ukrainian or Polish. "This man is only a recent arrival to Warsaw. He had just come fresh from Paris. Why would the French be so foolish as to trust him with this message?"

"Perhaps," Bohun speculated, "because they needed many riders. They may be marshaling their troops for a grand offensive and need every fighting soldier they can muster."

"Yet, you say you cannot read French?" asked the officer interrogating the courier.

"What is that supposed to mean?" asked Bohun.

The officer looked at Bohun like the wolf that had just devoured the prized calf. "Surely you are aware of what this message says?"

"No," Bohun admitted, "we have not the slightest idea. It was just fortunate that we overran our horses and they needed to be watered at about the same time this courier did along the creek."

"Well," the officer replied, "you know the old proverb, *Luck would not have happened without misfortune's help.*"

"So what is the answer to the great mystery?" asked Bohun.

"Not such an important thing," said the officer mockingly, "only that Napoleon is attempting to lure General Bennigsen and the bulk of the Russian army into a massive trap and by doing so to destroy them all at Thorn."

"Nyet, nepravda," replied Bohun.

"Yes, my friend, it is indeed true," the officer said, "or at least that is truly what the message says. It is a copy of orders sent out to all the marshals serving Napoleon. They are to lure Bennigsen to Thorn, and once the general is committed there, the French reserves under Napoleon's personal command will drive north from Warsaw and cut the army off and destroy it. General Buxhowden is in the process of assessing if this is false information, intended for us to capture, and to be found only as a means to deceive us."

Bohun was amazed at their fortune in having stumbled upon such a significant message. He pondered how they had happened upon the rider and determined it to be far too haphazard to have been set up in advance.

"There is no way that rider could have anticipated our watering our mounts at that exact spot!" Bohun said. "We must get this information to General Bennigsen. It must be true. From where was his last report sent?"

The officer looked at the leader of these Cossacks and weighed whether to share that crucial information with him. Then, he decided that it could do no harm, as they were too far east to share it with anyone, especially the French.

"General Bennigsen has been advancing steadily toward Thorn. Ney spotted and attacked his flank, but it was only a skirmish, and the marshal afterward retreated south. At Mohrungen, he encountered Marshal Bernadotte's First Corps, which was more formidable in size, but still far too weak to resist the mass of the Tsar's army. Instead, the French Marshal Bernadotte fights only rear-guard actions as he retreats toward Thorn."

"Slowing but not stopping General Bennigsen's troops," Bohun noted, "leading him into the trap as these orders say, but allowing Napoleon enough time to get his forces in place to spring the final attack. It all makes sense."

"Yes," the officer said, "I believe so, and as you say, messengers will need to be sent to General Bennigsen."

"Send my Cossacks," Bohun demanded. "It was our luck to stumble upon this. It should be our honor to carry it forward to General Bennigsen."

Chapter 5:
A Trap Too Soon Sprung

apoleon and his marshals were encamped in East Prussia awaiting to unleash one final attack upon Bennigsen's eastward-moving forces. With him were Marshals Ney, Soult, Davout, and Augereau as they convened a council of war.

"What I do not understand," Ney said at the table in the command tent, "is why the Russians put Bennigsen, a German, a Hanoverian at that, in charge of their forces replacing Kamensky."

"The Russian General Kamensky was an old, timid fool," Napoleon said, "look how easily we dispatched the Tsar's forces placed under him at Pułtusk. Once the real fighting began, Kamensky could do nothing other than retreat to Bialystok, where he would be close enough to the Russian border that he could readily slip across to safety. Even young Alexander could see this."

Several of the marshals gathered thought that the Battle of Pułtusk in late December had hardly been the complete victory that Napoleon had declared it to be. Still, the Russian General Kamensky had retreated from the field of battle, allowing Napoleon to declare he had won. In reality, most of the marshals considered it to have been much more of a stalemate.

"Kamensky retreated from us," the Emperor went on, "just as that other general of theirs-the fat, one-eyed old fool, General Kutuzov-had done after his defeat at Ulm. But even the Russians cannot run forever, as Kutuzov was soon to learn at Austerlitz."

"Many have said that it was Tsar Alexander himself," Marshal Davout, the *"Iron Marshal,"* interjected, "who forced Kutuzov to take the field at Austerlitz. Kutuzov was opposed to the idea, but had to comply as both the Tsar and his Polish Foreign Minister, Adam Czartoryski, were present at Austerlitz, well, at least nearby at their headquarters in Olmütz."

"Well, my brave French Marshals," Napoleon replied, "therein lies the secret to our success. It lies in my trust of each of you, Frenchmen through and through. As well, my Foreign Minister, Talleyrand, is a Frenchman throughout every fiber of his deceitful little crippled body."

The marshals laughed out loud at the Emperor's description of the absent Foreign Minister, but Napoleon ignored their mirth and continued.

"By comparison, the young Russian Tsar depends heavily on these generals of German descent absorbed into the Russian army in his father's time and even before. These so-called Russian Generals, such as Bennigsen, Buxhowden, and even their Field Marshal Barclay de Tolly, are all actually of German descent, even though they have long served in the Russian army's ranks. Still, Russia is not their native land. Thus, the young Alexander has important advisers who are from foreign lands. His Russian-born generals, such as Kutuzov and Kamensky, apparently only know how to withdraw. Alexander recognizes this weakness in them, so instead he turns to those German officers already in the Russian ranks to lead his army. But also, he allows himself to be advised in matters of State by the Pole, Adam Czartoyski. Can you imagine my turning the affairs of France over to an Austrian or an Italian? Of course not. Impossible!"

Each Marshal of the French Empire present had the exact same thought upon hearing these words uttered by the Emperor - that Napoleon himself took no advice from anyone, for anything not forthcoming from his own fruitful mind was suspect.

All else was considered by the Emperor to be inferior, even those sage bits of wisdom supplied from the best minds of Frenchmen, like his great Minister Talleyrand.

It was then that an urgent messenger arrived. Napoleon was handed a dispatch from the front and read it to himself.

Napoleon dismissed the messenger before saying to his gathered marshals, "It appears my last few words may have been unfortunately prophetic. For now, it appears even the commanding General Bennigsen has adopted the Russian trait of withdrawing from his engagements, as he has now done with Marshal Bernadotte. He is no longer pushing east to Thorn, but instead is withdrawing, heading further north, deeper into East Prussia. It appears he has somehow become aware of our trap."

"Then what shall we do, Sire?" asked Marshal Soult.

"We pursue! We pursue northward and catch up to the Russians. Eventually, we will force ourselves upon them and they will have no other option than to stand and fight like soldiers against *La Grande Armée*!"

Chapter 6:
A Symphony of Sorrows

Magdalena trudged through January's ankle-deep snow as she walked home from her day's work as governess at the Countess Marie Walewska's elegant townhome. While the Walewski family's Warsaw residence could not truly be called a palace, as their country estate at Walewice indeed could, it exuded far more opulence than the comfortable and well-appointed townhome in which Magdalena and her family resided. The usage of that property was thanks solely to the magnanimous generosity of Princess Izabela Czartoryska.

Magdalena shook the last clinging clumps of snow from her shoes and legs before she dropped down defeatedly onto the sofa closest to the roaring fire. Her daughter-in-law, Maya, was nursing her cousin Bohun's infant son there. Despite the tenderness of that delicate moment, a frigid heaviness followed Magdalena into the room, one so cold that even the wildly flickering flames that licked away at the cut logs failed to melt it away.

"What is the matter, *Matka?*" Maya asked. She had taken to addressing the woman who had given birth to her husband by the Polish word for mother after the two had moved to Warsaw to live together. It was a sign of her deepest respect, not only for all Magdalena had done for her personally, but for all she had endured throughout a hard and troubled life.

It pained Maya to admit to herself that the very worst of this woman's sorrows had come at the insidious hands of her own father - the late Duke Władyslaw Sdanowicz - who had so harshly ruled over all the peasants upon his *folwark* at Wieliczka. Her husband's mother was one of those, then known simply as Magda.

"I feel that this shell of a world we live in," Magdalena replied to Maya's question as she stared into the flames, "is about to collapse around us. Have you ever seen a serpent devour a bird's egg? It swallows it whole. Well, I feel we are already in the belly of the beast, only the illusion of the shell around us has not yet been dissolved away."

"I do not quite understand," answered Maya, wincing as the infant child of her cousin painfully suckled at her tender nipple.

"I have today learned that your husband, my Marek, has rejoined Emperor Napoleon in his quest to do battle with the Russians. They have headed north into East Prussia to do so."

"How could you possibly know this?" Maya asked. "I thought there were to be no battles until the spring thaws came."

"I know because it was shared with me by the Countess," Magdalena said, "as she also is despondent. It appears the Russians could not wait until the warming of spring to move against the French. Nor could our Marek resist joining Napoleon in response."

"I do not understand," Maya continued, "how the Countess might have come upon this information. Did she overhear the Emperor's plans being discussed by her husband, the Count?"

"My child," Magdalena said while turning her head away from the fire to face her, "you are so blissfully unaware. The Countess has been asked to give herself to the Emperor, who has become smitten with her. The elders of Poland have proposed, no, demanded that the young Marie lie down by Napoleon's side so that our country may soon rise again - a request that the Countess rejected out of hand, but her decision was not accepted."

Maya could not believe what she was being told. It was not that long ago that the beautiful young Countess had married the seventy-plus-year-old Count Athanasius Colonna-Walewski. Marie Walewska was a righteous, well-respected woman. She had given Count Walewski a child, a son. How could anyone possibly ask her to debase herself so disreputably in this way?

"Nie prawda," Maya said in shock, "her refusal was rejected even by her own husband? I cannot believe that a man so prominent in the community as the Count would allow this to occur."

"Yes, it is true. Even her own old, decrepit husband," Magdalena replied, her voice ringed with a hollow echo of sorrow. "These rich old men only care about their own interests, saving what they can: their country palaces, their fine city homes. That filthy old Count allows his beautiful young wife to be taken to the Emperor like some sacrificial animal as an offering of appeasement. It is disgusting."

"Yes, truly disgusting," Maya agreed. "What kind of world will our little ones inherit? What a mess we have made of things, *Matka…"*

"No, my darling," Magdalena added, "the world we live in has been tainted not by our doing, but by the evil lust of men. Both you and I have been touched darkly by it. Our country was lost to it. Never place blame on yourself for their deceitful doings."

"This is terribly horrible news! Now, I must fear anew for Marek's very safety," Maya said as if the impact of Magdalena's words regarding her husband had just settled upon her. "And how cruel that I must hear this burdensome report from your already overtaxed heart. Are you aware that your son refuses to even meet with me anymore? He is so disgusted with us as a couple."

"As he is also angry with me," Magdalena added. "If only Ewelina had not betrayed my sorrowful secret to him, none of this would have happened. Is my sister-in-law here now?"

"No," Maya said, turning her head away and toward the suckling child, not out of the infant's need for her attention, but more out of a heaviness of incredible shame.

The weight of that shame was hung on her during her last meeting with her husband, Marek, on the banks of the Vistula. There, he had shared with her the awful truth regarding his father. It had been spewed so venomously on him by his Aunt Ewelina. She had told him that the peasant Bronislaw, Ewelina's own brother, whom Marek had loved so dearly and known as his *Tata,* was not his father at all. Instead, his father was the Duke Sdanowicz of the *folwark* on which they had been raised - the same man who was Maya's father. The Duke had forced himself upon Magda, the peasant girl who then worked in his manor house.

That fact meant Maya and Marek were half-siblings. Marek could not deal with that crippling, inconvenient truth. They had shared a childhood together, he being the peasant boy, she the Duke's cherished, protected daughter. They fell in love even before they knew what love was. Much later, in Paris, at the time of the Emperor's coronation, both, unaware of this well-kept family secret, had conceived a child, Czesław, together.

Czesław was a beautiful but quiet child. Marek had only recently even come to know that he had a son, and was so pleased that he had become a father. Then, upon learning the harsh reality of the true identity of his own father, Marek's thoughts became consumed with Czesław being a spawn of incest. Marek told Maya that despite his love for her, he could no longer be with her. He could no longer condone the curse set upon their family - to live together as man and wife when, in reality, she was his half-sister. Even though it was no fault of her own, he knew it to be an offense against God. Against all that is good. Marek promised to support them financially, as much as he could on his military pay, but still he vowed to return to Paris after this current campaign was over. He swore never again to see Maya or their child, Czesław.

The Russians had put her offending uncle's head on a pike at the Battle of Maciejowice, while she was still pregnant with Władek. That was over a decade ago; the child was now eleven. But to Marek, she thought, their older son was just one more reason to abandon her. Sadly, Władek was so infatuated with the warrior he thought to be his father that he demanded to be called Marek after him. Władek no longer answered to his given name.

Prior to Marek's arrival for Christmas, Maya thought she had finally achieved what her heart had always desired most. Marek had agreed to accept her as his wife and Władek as his own son to the outside world, at least on the pretense of a false church wedding document. He had always known Władek was illegitimate, but with the recent revelation of his own father's identity, Marek could no longer engage in this charade. Sadly, it only hardened his heart more toward the child that Maya loved so.

"Is my sister-in-law Ewelina here?" Magdalena asked again, having lost her first query to Maya's introspection.

"I'm sorry, *Matka*. No," Maya replied with a snap of her attention, "Ewelina has gone for a walk. She takes such long walks every day in this wicked, bitter cold that sometimes I think she is merely tempting God to strike her down with sickness to take her from this world of misery in which she dwells."

"Yet she delights in sharing that misery by poisoning my own son against me, and your husband against you, my dear."

"She has had too much sorrow for any single woman to be asked to bear," Maya said sympathetically.

"Have not we all?" Magdalena muttered under her breath. She then raised her voice and said, "Ewelina has assured to that! I fear what other ways she will find to attack us both, but I most dread that Marek himself will somehow suffer terribly at her hand. She has become incredibly bitter, and that animus has unleashed a fierce cruelty within her. I have such an impending sense of disaster hanging over me; it shrouds my soul in darkness."

Maya moved the infant away from her breast to her shoulder, where she patted his back tenderly.

"Praise be to God," she said to lighten the tone, "that we live here under the generosity of the Princess Czartoryska, and that you have your position as governess for Countess Walewska. Yet, you say the Countess herself was in deep despair at the Emperor's leaving to do battle with the Russians. I would think his departure from Warsaw might bring the Countess some relief from the burden of being expected to lie with him at the Royal Castle."

Magdalena looked at the infant child resting upon her daughter-in-law's shoulder. She reached out to stroke the tender skin of his cheek. Then, she asked Maya about her older son.

"Forgive my being so bold, Maya, but do you love your Władek even though he was forced upon you against your will?"

"You know that I do," the younger woman answered. "Have I not shown him great love while I have lived with you?"

"Yes, you have, always, my child," Magdalena answered, "just as I love my Marek, who was also forced upon me. I am ashamed to admit it now, but while I carried him, I often wondered if I could ever bring myself to truly love him. But love is something that cannot be denied. Not by the rationality of social laws or by the propriety of so-called righteous men. Thankfully, our hearts love not because it is right or wrong given any particular social conventions regarding the two souls involved, but rather because our hearts are filled with a special tenderness so strong and so infinite that its love can never be fully contained."

Maya's eyes teared up as she recalled her own doubts, those she once harbored while carrying her firstborn, her Władek. She, too, had feared she might never have feelings for the child growing within her as it was conceived under a cold and forceful lust, not wrapped warmly in the purity of romantic love. Once the boy was born, however, any question of holding this sin against him vanished away with the sight of the child's innocence.

"I understand precisely, but do not understand what all this might have to do with the young Countess Walewska," Maya said.

"Because," Magdalena drew in a deep consoling breath, and only upon expelling found the words she needed to explain, "the Countess Marie has shared with me that she is falling in love with the Emperor. She never expected it, with her liaisons with him being forced upon her in the way that they were by her countrymen, but nonetheless, it is so. He treats her so tenderly that she feels he actually cares for her, even saying that if he were her husband, he would never allow her to leave his side."

"Such hypocrisy! It was he who demanded that the Polish elders send her to him! Does she not see the irony of this? You say she has only been with him for a few weeks," Maya gasped. "She fell in love that fast?"

"The heart demands what the heart desires," Magdalena said. "There can be simply no denying it."

"Unless the one your heart desires denies you first," Maya countered, thinking of her situation with her husband, Marek.

Chapter 7: Day One
The Battle of Eylau

Bennigsen committed his Russian forces to engage at Mohrungen with the French Marshal Bernadotte's First Corps on the 25th of January. The Russian general afterward began to pursue the French in the direction of Thorn. When the Cossacks arrived with the intercepted Imperial orders, they were presented to the Russian commander just in time for him to disengage from the French and escape the trap being laid by Napoleon. In fact, if not for the Cossacks under Bohun, the bulk of the Tsar's forces would most likely have been decimated.

General Bennigsen retreated with his army northward, skirmishing only lightly with the *Grande Armée* as he did so. But when he came to the crossroads village of Preussisch-Eylau, north of Heilsberg along the approach to Königsberg, Bennigsen knew it was the location where he would make his stand. That engagement would begin almost accidentally on the afternoon of the seventh of February, and the battle that would grow from it would carry over throughout the full next day. These would prove to be two of the most cruel and intense days of fighting for both armies, not only in terms of the vicious brutality of conflict, but also in having to endure the most wicked wrath of winter imaginable.

General Bennigsen knew, as he first saw the village cemetery which rose on a slight knoll overlooking open fields in all directions, that Eylau would be where he would force Napoleon to fail to taste victory for the first time in battle.

The massive Russian army would retreat no further. As it was to turn out, the general's thoughts had never been more prophetic, although the final result of the battle to come would surely not be what Bennigsen had envisioned at the time.

Bennigsen gave orders for the placement of his sixty-three thousand troops and their more than four hundred pieces of artillery surrounding the village. He awaited the arrival of General Anton Wilhelm von L'Estocq, the seventy-year-old Prussian who commanded another nine thousand soldiers. But Bennigsen did not realize that Bonaparte had, by then, already given Marshal Ney orders to pursue and harass those same Prussian forces. The Emperor's order was to prevent General L'Estocq, at all costs, from joining up with the Russian forces. Ney had fifteen thousand men at his disposal. He tracked the Prussians through the snows and forests up along the Baltic coast.

His fellow marshals later jested with Ney that this dogging of L'Estocq had been Napoleon's punishment for disregarding his orders by moving from the Emperor's assigned area. Yet, despite Napoleon's decrying the marshal's impertinence, the others clearly saw that it was only Ney's impulsive move that resulted in his stumbling upon the enemy's unexpected winter movement in the first place. Ney foiled Bennigsen's stealthy attack, which surely would have wreaked havoc upon unsuspecting French forces at Thorn and cut crucial supply lines upon which they all depended.

In early February, Napoleon lost sight of his enemy's massive army. He chased the Russians north toward Allenstein, where he learned that the Russians were just northeast of the city. He pressed to trap them in the town of Ionkovo. While a brief but fierce battle was fought there, the Russians once more slipped away. Not until the seventh of February would Napoleon stumble upon their waiting forces at the village of Preussisch-Eylau. There, a clumsy, accidental engagement would precipitate into one of the fiercest and most devastating battles of the Napoleonic Wars.

On the afternoon of the seventh of February, the temperature dropped to well below freezing. The skies hung heavy with pregnant gray clouds looming overhead, but yielding only intermittent snow showers despite threatening an impending blizzard. Marshal Soult's forces secured the gates of the town of Eylau, not realizing the Russian army had taken up positions just yards beyond it. The Emperor's advanced belongings, those to be readied for Napoleon's field headquarters, were delivered to the cemetery ridge just east of the village itself. This spot was selected because the rise of the hill there afforded views of all the surrounding open areas. As always, the Emperor's possessions were protected by an advance unit of the trusted Imperial Guard.

Marek Zaczek was assigned to that protective detail that day. They had just delivered the Emperor's effects and were overseeing their unpacking when Marek and the rest of the Imperial Guard detail were overrun by a Russian patrol coming out of the cemetery itself. A struggle engaged with the Russians as the Imperial Guard closed in around the enemy patrol. Yet as they did, another Russian force emerged, and the Imperial Guard was quickly outnumbered.

"Zaczek," a voice cried out, "go and retrieve Soult's men from within the gates of the town, or we will all be cut down."

As the Russians moved *en masse,* Marek spurred his mount and rode to the village's main gates. He began to draw fire as his silhouette dashed along the cemetery ridge toward Soult's men. Arriving there, he urged the commanders of Soult's Corps to come to the aid of the Imperial Guard, which they did with great haste. However, by the time all arrived, more Russians had engaged, and a major life-or-death battle was taking place within the cemetery among the headstones. As he returned to the cemetery, Marek's horse was shot out from under him. He was fortunate to be able to crawl over to take refuge behind a great marker erected nearby. It proved to be his only cover from the firing of Russian rifles.

Marek raised his eyes to look upon the marker to discover a prominent Germanic name, Hans Schmoeckel. *Thank God for these proud Prussians, descendants of the determined Teutonic Knights,* he thought, protected as he was from the enemy fire only by the bulk of the massive, ornate headstone. Marek thought, *I am most grateful that Herr Hans Schmoeckel was successful enough a merchant to afford such a large headstone.*

Soon after, the Imperial Guard, accompanied by Soult's still arriving troops, drove the Russians back from the ridge by attaching bayonets. The Emperor's advanced effects had once again been secured, but not before the Russian soldiers had enough time to pore over them and pilfer some personal souvenirs.

What became clear to all parties at this time was that the Russians were encamped just beyond the village of Eylau in great numbers. Orders were given to fight house to house to drive out all the remaining of the Tsar's troops from within the village itself.

Darkness and the temperature had both begun to fall dramatically. As they did, the French troops fought with fervor. They realized that if they did not clear the village's buildings, they would be forced to bivouac out in the open elements, where a very real threat of freezing to death awaited them.

While this fighting took place, accidentally triggered as it was, wave after wave of French forces continued to pour into the village from the south. The fighting for control of its structures became bloody and intense, but the continual addition of French reinforcements from the late-arriving corps succeeded in the French securing what would become their main encampment.

Marshals Augereau, Murat, and Soult took the village just prior to the Emperor's arrival. By the end of the first day's fighting, the net comparison of force levels was still decidedly in favor of the Russians. They had amassed some sixty-three thousand troops around Eylau, and by day's end, Napoleon would have only forty-five thousand men in place.

The next day, Marshal Davout was expected to arrive with another fifteen thousand troops, bringing the Emperor's total to near sixty thousand, on par with the Russian strength, so long as Marshal Ney proved capable of keeping the nine thousand Prussian troops under General L'Estocq at bay near the Baltic shores.

Napoleon was surprised to be at a disadvantage as night fell. Where were Marshal Bernadotte and his First Corps, whose unexpected absence resulted in the Russians' having an unexpected but decided advantage?

As it was, Bernadotte and his First Corps would not arrive until two days after all fighting had concluded. This was because the orders for his corps to deploy had been those intercepted by the Cossacks. Still, even without Bernadotte's First Corps, Napoleon believed he had enough forces in place to win the battle, so long as Marshal Davout arrived the next day as planned. Also, Marshal Ney must keep L'Estcoq's Prussian forces away from the battle.

That first day of fighting was brutally severe, with each side losing some four thousand men to death, injury, or capture. In the conditions faced overnight, many, if not most, of those wounded on the battlefield would freeze to death in a slow, torturous cycle of excruciating pain and numbing frostbite.

Whereas the French proved successful in clearing the village, they drove the Russians out into the open fields surrounding Eylau. There, the Tsar's troops were forced to bivouac in the open freezing fields with no campfires, fearing the light of these would only draw cannon fire from the French. As if to make matters worse, the skies began to unrelentingly pelt driving snow on a continuing basis. The net effect of this was the severe dampening of all sound, creating a crystalline silence pierced only by the pathetic intermittent low moans of the wounded combatants from both sides as they lie exposed in the darkening fields around Eylau. The cries of these men went unanswered, for the most part, as they slowly froze to death.

Chapter 8: Day Two
The Battle of Eylau

Napoleon surveyed the fields surrounding his forces at Eylau as the sun rose, surprised to find the Russians neatly set in multiple lines of artillery and infantry stretched out in layered arcs three miles long before him. No sooner had the darkness yielded to the exposing light of dawn, the Russian cannons opened up with a most impressive yet primitive volley of artillery fire. This drew the response of the French guns, and thus began one of the most destructive artillery barrages of the Napoleonic Wars. Each side bombarded the other for hours, as the fresh blankets of overnight snow did its best to swallow whole the echoes, if not the thunder of the guns themselves.

The French were outnumbered as Marshal Davout had still not yet arrived, and Marshal Bernadotte and his First Corps were not to be found as the Emperor had expected. Still, there was a fortunate, if unintended, advantage held by the French. Their Russian enemy's lines were tightly formed and placed one behind the other. Their soldiers were so densely packed that the French cannonballs could not fail to do great damage. Conversely, even though the French were mostly bottled up within the village, their forces were scattered among various buildings and structures. This failed to provide as dense a target, mitigating much of the collateral damage from the discharge of the Russian guns. Still, the great numerical advantage in the number of cannons possessed by the Russians seemed enough to offset this tactical benefit held by the more dispersed French.

As the morning wore on and the massive artillery barrage continued, Napoleon sought to penetrate the center of the Russian lines. He sent an engagement of cavalry out from the village towards the nearest Russian batteries. This column was comprised of Marshal Augereau's Seventh Corps and a division of Marshal Soult's Fourth Corps under the leadership of the Comte St. Hilaire.

Marshal Charles Pierre François Augereau was one of the longest-serving of Napoleon's marshals. He had been with Bonaparte since the Italian campaign in early 1796 and was, in fact, present when Zaczek defected across the bridge at Lodi. The Emperor had great faith in Augereau's leadership abilities to cut through the confusion and disarray so prevalent on the battlefield.

Severely ill with fever during the previous day's engagements, Marshal Augereau had to be helped onto his saddle on the morning of that second day. St. Hilaire commanded his unit alongside Augereau to the French marshal's right. Even as the cannonballs continued to ballistically arc overhead, the French cavalry units moved valiantly toward the awaiting Russian lines. It was then that the inexplicable will of God intervened.

As both cavalry units departed, the heaviest snows of the battle descended upon them in near-blizzard conditions. St. Hilaire was successful in navigating through it to find and engage the Russian lines, but Marshal Augereau veered off to his left in the heaviest throes of the whiteout. Snow-blind, he catastrophically led his forces into the *"no man's land"* between the center of the French and Russian lines, where the heaviest concentrations of the artillery units were placed.

Marshal Augereau's forces soon found themselves beneath the thrusts of the volleys of the overhead cannonade from both encampments. Augereau remained unaware of his critical mistake until the heaviest of the snows began to recede. As the white veils of precipitation abated, Augereau was aghast to find his cavalry immediately in front of a bank of some seventy Russian cannons.

The Russians quickly lowered their guns and opened fire with canister shot, obliterating the French soldiers on horseback. Augereau was severely wounded in the arm.

One unit caught in that melee, the *14th Ligne,* was unable to fall back and literally fought to nearly the last man. All that was eventually found of them was an overrun *Battalion Carré* of dead bodies. This left St. Hilaire's Fourth Corps unit alone to engage the Russian flank. With Augereau's forces peeled away, St. Hilaire had virtually no effect in penetrating the enemy's lines.

After Marshal Augereau's disastrous veering off course, with the French center having been breached, all looked dire for *La Grande Armée* that morning at Eylau. As Augereau's cavalry, what was left of them, fought to return to the French lines, the Russian infantry seized the advantage and advanced behind them. As the Tsar's infantry broke through the French center, an immediate and deadly problem arose, imperiling the very life of the Emperor.

Marek Zaczek had not participated in the tragic cavalry charge, as his unit was assigned to Napoleon's Imperial Guard, which the Emperor held jealously in reserve. It formed a last ring of defense around the Emperor, who by then had taken to the bell tower of the cemetery's church, using it as a makeshift observation post. With the Russian infantry breaking through the French lines, the Imperial Guard was all that stood between, or in this case below, their Emperor and his being captured. Napoleon faced not only the aspect of a first defeat, but also of being abducted, which would end his aspirations of controlling all of Continental Europe.

Ringed around the base of that church, the Imperial Guard fought desperately to save Napoleon from the advancing enemy troops. It is believed that as many as nine thousand Russians surged through its snow-covered cemetery headstones. Marek found himself, for the second day in a row, in hand-to-hand combat with the Russians. The dead from the day before lay at the combatants' feet, still having not been cleared away.

The Imperial Guard held off the enemy just long enough for reinforcements to arrive. Marek and the others thrust with outstretched bayonets, impaling Russian infantry, who soon found themselves cut off and isolated. In the end, as many as two thousand of the enemy perished there.

The breach through the center of the French lines had been halted, but as for Marek, it was the first time in his service to Napoleon that he was nearly certain that his own life was about to be taken from him. The myth of French invincibility was shattered in him and among all the soldiers of *La Grande Armée* that day.

If the Battle of Pułtusk in December truly was Napoleon's first failure to gain a decisive victory in combat, then Eylau at that moment threatened to become the Emperor's first truly outright defeat on the battlefield.

With having just barely survived his center being broken outright, and with Augereau's cavalry still being cut to pieces, Napoleon turned to his brother-in-law, Marshal Joachim Murat, who commanded the massive reserve cavalry, and said wryly to him,

"Are you going to let those fellows devour us?" [3]

The comment prompted one of the largest and most destructive charges of cavalry ever assembled. Murat personally led nearly eleven thousand men on horseback to attack the Russian lines. The shining metal breastplates of the French Cuirassiers on their heavy mounts must have seemed as imposing as the Spanish Conquistadors of old as they thundered toward the Russian lines.

------

[3] "The Battle of Eylau: A Massacre Without Results," Vince Hawkins, Warfare History Network

The Cuirassiers were led by an advance of Dragoons and other heavy cavalry, which initially broke through the enemy lines. They slashed through that opening to wreak death and havoc behind the Russian front. Even though the Tsar's army became severely penetrated in places, it held out nonetheless. There was no catastrophic collapse. There was no frantic fleeing retreat, as the Russians fought with discipline and valor until their own cavalry arrived to engage the French charge. The lines of horsemen formed and reformed in a dynamic, wrenching fashion. Pockets of French cavalry were soon encircled, and secondary charges had to be mounted to free these units, to give them a fighting chance to battle their way back to safety. Amongst this horrific fighting, Colonel Lepic of the Mounted Grenadiers of the Guard, his men ducking their heads under a withering crossfire, urged them on by saying,

"Heads up, by God! Those are bullets - not turds."[4]

Hour after hour, more infantry and cavalry from both sides fell in battle upon the snow-covered grounds, from the cemetery ridge controlled by the French deep into the lines of the Russians in the open fields. Amongst the artillery barrages and the slashing strikes of the cavalry's sabres, those who fell wounded would slowly have their lives drained from them. The icy battlefield seemed to have a ghoulish spectre's insatiable hunger for souls.

While all this occurred, Marshal Davout's Fifth Corps began arriving on the Russian left flank. Thanks to the disruption of Murat's immense cavalry charge, the battle had balanced out, but still with no significant advantage to either side. However, this would change with the arrival of Davout, known amongst the French forces as the *"Iron Marshal."* The arrival of Marshal Davout's forces had been precisely what Napoleon had been awaiting, along with Marshal Bernadotte, who still had not arrived due to his orders having been intercepted by the Cossack scouts.

---

[4] The Campaigns of Napoleon, Volume II, David Chandler, 1966, p. 169

As the bulk of Davout's fifteen-thousand-strong Fifth Corps forces began to arrive, they took control of the Russian left flank. They were able to drive the Russians back, overtaking critical high ground known as the *"Kreege Burge"* and then commandeering the Russian guns upon it. Davout even advanced deeply enough to threaten Bennigsen's command post before being driven back by Russian forces. Fighting between Marshal Davout's Fifth Corps and the Russians continued throughout the rest of the day on the Russian left flank, at times imperiling either side.

Late in the day, the nine thousand Prussian troops under General L'Estocq slipped past Ney's Sixth Corps along the Baltic coast and marched eight miles to join the main battle at Eylau. This gave the Russian side a slight but fresh advantage, which they pressed to threaten Davout's forces with imminent destruction. Their saving grace was the arrival of Marshal Ney's Sixth Corps, which had trailed the Prussians to the battlefield. Ney's fifteen thousand forces proved to be the decisive factor that convinced Bennigsen he no longer had any real opportunity to win the battle. Darkness descended, the fighting was halted, and both sides suffered from near exhaustion.

This marked the end of a particularly bloody two-day engagement. Both sides were thought to have casualties of over twenty thousand soldiers. As for the few new Polish forces, those who fought their first battle for Napoleon over those two days were reminded of their homeland's national colors every time they looked down to see the bright, scarlet-red blood streaked across the pure white fields of snow. For these most recently assigned Poles, Eylau would be their first taste of war, but far from their last.

Perhaps the wanton squander of the debacle that was Eylau was best captured by Marshal Ney himself. As he surveyed the battlefield after all fighting had ceased, he saw that death was the only true victor, having claimed what seemed to be an innumerable number of French, Russian, Polish, and Cossack souls.

The frozen battlegrounds were strewn so pathetically with dead and wounded that Ney, disgusted by the mayhem and waste of life, famously called out,

"Quel massacre! Et sans résultat!"

("What a massacre! And without result!")[5]

---

[5] *Souvenirs Militairies de 1804 à 1814* by French General Raymond Aimery Philippe Joseph de Montesquiou-Fezensac (1863).

After fourteen hours of exhaustive battle on that second fiercely frigid day, after the daring charges and counter-charges of both sides' cavalry, after the loss of startling levels of Russian and French infantry, and after the near capture of both Napoleon and Bennigsen, both leaders' lines remained arranged much the same at that day's close as they had been at its beginning.

That night, under the cover of darkness, Bennigsen pulled his remaining troops from the battle. Under the protective guard of Cossack units - Bohun's and many thousands of others - the Russians withdrew northward into East Prussia. Deprived of a third day of bloodying those pristine white fields cleansed by the overnight snowfall, Napoleon knew his army was in no condition to pursue the escaping enemy. Instead, he would be forced to settle by declaring the battle to be a crucial French victory. He does so in one of his first notes after the battle to Talleyrand:

"Monsieur le Prince de Bénévent (Talleyrand's title), it is two o'clock in the morning; I'm tired; I can only write you one word. Marshal Duroc will inform you of the victory won yesterday over the Russian army."[6]

Bennigsen would do much the same as he presented the battle's results before his glory-hungry Tsar - a dozen captured French Eagles (those standards in the style carried long ago by Roman Legions). The Russian commander declared these as proof of Napoleon's horrific losses, while he downplayed his own, as:

"...a strategic achievement in diluting the forces of the French."

To which Tsar Alexander replied,

"It was your destiny to earn glory by defeating the one who has never been defeated."[7]

---

[6] Napoleon to Talleyrand, 9 February (2 AM), 1807, *Foundation Napoléon Archives*

[7] "Napoleon's Costly Victory at Eylau" by Victor Kamenir, Warfare History Network.

Napoleon would not admit defeat, just the contrary. He would claim victory at Eylau, which was tactically true given Bennigsen's withdrawal, but that was strategically insignificant. The victory was pyrrhic at best, with his own losses rattling the Emperor. In his later correspondence to Josephine after the battle, Napoleon was uncharacteristically subdued:

"My darling, there was a great battle yesterday. The victory remained with me, but I lost many people. The loss of the enemy, which is even more considerable, does not console me. Finally, I am writing these two lines to you myself, although I am very tired, to tell you that I am in good health and that I love you."[8]

Napoleon scribbled these words of amour to his wife even though he would soon direct his Marshal of the Palace, General Duroc, to find a field headquarters suitable for bringing along his mistress, Marie Walewska. His close call with fate at the church required the distraction of the Countess' attention more than ever.

Despite how the Emperor chose to frame the *"victory,"* his marshals all knew Ney's assessment to be the most accurate. It was merely another stalemate, just as Pułtusk and Gołymin had been. Yet, one much larger in scope, stealing away between a quarter to a third of the French forces, with similar percentages lost on the enemy's side as well. Eylau was a horrendous conflict that unnecessarily sacrificed the lives of fearless soldiers on both sides in large numbers for no perceptible outcome. It truly was a *"massacre without result,"* except that the veil of Napoleon's invincibility, ripped open by the draws at Pułtusk and Gołymin just before the new year, was in February completely shredded. After the massive waste of human life over those two insufferable frostbitten days along the open fields and cemetery ridge of the crossroad village of Preussisch-Eylau, the myth of Napoleon's invulnerability was exposed.

---

[8] Napoleon to Josephine, 9 February (3 AM), 1807, *Foundation Napoléon Archives*

Figure 14: Emperor Napoleon at The Battle of Eylau (Gros)

Part Two:

A Pause for Reflection:
Echoes of Eylau

"It is better to be unhappy

and know the worst,

than to be happy in a fool's paradise."

Fyodor Dostoevsky

Afterward, during that February, Marek recovered from the Battle of Eylau totally disoriented. What had been gained by this stalemated massacre? So many men with whom he had shared in victory after victory, at Ulm, Austerlitz, Jena, and throughout Europe, died on those snowy fields of East Prussia, for seemingly nothing. No real victory was achieved, only two days of slaughter after which the enemy sulked away like a weary child into the black of night. That horrendous waste of life - Russian, French, and Polish - pierced Marek's mind, with the sounds of their dying, their moaning, becoming a morbid cacophony drowning out even the thunderous bursts of cannons. So many souls squandered to their eternal fate, and for what purpose? Just so one man, the Emperor of France, could declare himself superior to the young upstart Tsar? So Bonaparte could finally punish the King and Queen of Prussia for daring to raise an army against him?

As Napoleon had predicted, General Bennigsen withdrew his forces from the field of battle at Eylau just after the end of the second day of fighting. After which, the Russian army hunkered down, inactive for the remaining winter months. When the weather warmed, they moved evasively like the surviving pieces of an inferior opponent's chess board - not yet in mate, but ever leery it would become their ultimate destiny. The Russians thus evaded *La Grande Armée* at every turn until they could eventually come across a situation that benefited themselves, in which they greatly outnumbered a smaller group of their opponent's forces. Perhaps then, and only then, might they attack to reverse their fortunes.

That proved to be the great distinction between Bennigsen and Napoleon - the Emperor did not avoid an even-up fight, but lived for the thrill of just such a confrontation. Napoleon saw each battle as a test of his skill, as a measure of his mettle as a field commander, and as a sounding of the sharpness of his strategies. He thrived on knowing that even though he had never been openly defeated in battle, it still remained a possible, disastrous fate.

Despite declaring it a victory, Napoleon remained shaken by the magnitude of his losses at Eylau. He had never come closer to defeat. He lingered over its corpse-ridden fields, not giving the order to evacuate until the 16th of February. While he would have loved to return to the Royal Castle on the Vistula at Warsaw to resume his tryst with Countess Marie Walewska, he knew he must stay in the field to remedy all that had gone wrong, not just on the battlefield, but within himself. Napoleon knew his army, of which a third may have been lost at Eylau, needed to be rebuilt. So, after reflecting on the spectre of near defeat for over a week, the *Grande Armée* finally vacated Eylau and headed to the town of Osteröde.

For Countess Walewska, the news wounded her heart. Marie had come to cherish her romantic liaisons with her Napoleon. It amazed her how soothing these hours with this man could be for her. Their richness made her aware of just how void of purpose her life had become. After all, Marie had been married off by her mother and her brothers to the aged *starosta of Warka,* Count Athenasius Colonna-Walewski, to clear the family's debts. At the time of their wedding in 1804, she had been merely eighteen years old, a child compared to her husband's sixty-eight years.

Wed to a man half a century her senior, Marie found herself robbed of the joys dreamt of by every flowering young girl; of igniting the infatuation of a dashing young man, of unbridling the passions within him, of releasing herself to be awash in the surge of his desire, and finally to surrender to its quivering crescendo of ecstasy. Instead, sold off like livestock; stolen from her were these dreams of charming out the romance of a young man's heart, and in return, allowing herself, body and soul, to be conquered.

Comfort was not an issue as her new but ancient husband was wealthy beyond near all compare. He had earlier been the chamberlain to the last King of Poland, Stanislaw Poniatowski, uncle of Prince Jozef Poniatowski, the current *de facto* leader of the subjugated Poles. By 1805, Marie had rendered her wifely duties to the aged Count and had given birth to his son.

The young Countess may have thought she was then as content as any beautiful mother who had all she could ever desire. Yet, Marie had so pathetically given up to necessity what her own heart wanted most - romance. So completely had her yearnings been suppressed that her heart became a victim of her own dutiful trap. It had become a gilded cage imprisoning a songbird that had never found reason to sing. A heart that had never stumbled upon a love to release the innocence of the child's mirth trapped within it.

Quickly, her contentment gave way to malaise. That *ennui* was pierced by the arrival of Napoleon. Not only did the news of his coming shatter the icy boredom of being entrapped in a Warsaw winter, but his spark ignited the kindling of Marie's heart. Was this man the adventurous leader she hoped would restore her country? Her long-suppressed desires, like grasses dried out during a severe drought, blazed into a raging wildfire until all that was left was a bed of throbbing red embers, only to cool in their desertion.

She had ridden out only months before, in December of 1806, to greet the Emperor as he stopped at the town of Blonie, just west of Warsaw. She only at that point wished most sincerely to thank him for being the savior who would liberate her homeland from the clutches of the three partitioning states: Prussia and Russia, with whom the Emperor still battled, and Austria, whom he had by then defeated. Yet, when she felt his gaze first fall upon her, she was framed in the warmth of her traveling fur. With her cheeks rouged with winter's crispness, her eyes ablaze with the promise of excitement, she sensed that the attention of Napoleon was instantly captured. Strangely, her natural, first reaction was to withdraw.

Then, in Warsaw, when this most powerful of all men did everything to convince her to come to him, she was caught in the torrents of swirling, conflicting emotions. The Emperor only wanted her for his pleasure, she was sure. *What kind of a man would make this demand of a virtuous married woman?* she wondered. *Are there not others in Warsaw more beautiful, more inclined for this unseemly service?* Her countrymen thought not.

Her first night with the Emperor completely changed her perception of the man. She had gone to the Royal Castle to tell him in person that she could not give herself to him in the way that he wished. When he so graciously convinced her that he only wanted her companionship and made no attempt to force himself upon her, those embers of her own heart ignited. *Perhaps I truly am the only woman in all of Poland that this man desires?*

Then she learned from General Duroc, who had befriended her, that the Emperor had written to Empress Josephine to forbid his wife to come to Warsaw. This news emboldened her. Marie came to relish the vitality of this man, still young at only thirty-eight years old. He courted her immodestly, caring not what the world around him thought, driven only by the fact that he needed her by his side. When his persistence of attention wore away at her, breathing like a bellows upon the embers of her desire already stoked, she eventually gave herself to him. In that moment, she felt love and pleasure in the touch of a man for the first time in her life.

Less than three months from that early morning rendezvous in the snow at Blonie, Napoleon had fully captured the heart of Marie Walewska. But even those days of bliss had an underlying edge of concern threaded through them. The very foes Marie had wished Napoleon to vanquish from the lands of Poland - the invading armies of Russia and Prussia - threatened to keep him away from her. When he did not return to Warsaw after Eylau, she longed only to return to his arms, to feel his breath fall softly on her like a fresh dew of spring to drive off the cruelty of winter.

Am I insane? she asked herself. *How long can this last? Either he will be killed outright on the battlefield, or even worse, he will defeat the enemies of my homeland, only to abandon me to return to France as a conquering hero and be embraced in the welcoming arms of Paris. Either way, I will be left alone to mourn his loss. This was a thought she could not bear.*

Only months before, she lived contentedly in the cold, but safe, clinical world of the Count. She dreaded to think of foregoing the fantasy of her impetuous imperial love; to return to the count's world would, by contrast, prove to be even more empty and sterile.

Marie could not resist the allure of Napoleon. She weighed every second away from him as a curse. In their relatively short time together, he had made her feel like the most important person in his dynamic world. Her heart had already surrendered that same status to him. The Countess could not abstain from his unceasing infatuation with her, as it was so much more consuming than what she had initially feared. The conqueror of Europe wanted her mind, her love, just as much as her body. He hungrily demanded her companionship and dialogue, something her own husband had never truly seemed to desire beyond the levels of simple courtesy.

Denied Napoleon's affections throughout February and March, Marie communicated with her lover by letter. The Emperor always made time to return her notes. As winter pressed on with Napoleon still at Osteröde, Warsaw began to fill with rumors of their relationship. It appears Napoleon may have feared these rumors might even reach Josephine in Paris.

Josephine herself took any reason she could to write to her husband. On the first of March, she wrote that she had been shaken after the ballet dancer Angélique Thérèse Aubry had a disfiguring accident in Paris playing Minerva in the ballet, *"Le Retour d'Ulysse,"* when a stage mechanism lowering her from a height collapsed. Josephine knew the woman had also been a model for her husband's favorite painter, Jacques-Louis David.

Perhaps the Empress saw this as an omen, with her husband in the role of Ulysses, attempting to return home after a lengthy campaign of battle, but delayed by fate and the wiles of goddesses. The Emperor replied to Josephine, fittingly, on the Ides of March:

"I received your letter of March 1st where I see that you
were very moved by the catastrophe of Minerve de l'Opéra.
I'm very happy to see you go out and have fun.
My health is very good, my business is going very well.
Do not give any credence to all the bad rumors that could be
spread. Never doubt my feelings, and be without any worry."[9]

So could Napoleon have been referring to rumors of his Polish mistress? It appears likely. Despite this, he was also sending letters to General Duroc, his Marshal of the Palace, to locate a field headquarters where the Countess Marie could safely and comfortably join him. Despite his reassurances to his wife, only two days later, Napoleon would write to Marie:

"Madam, I received two charming letters from you,
the feelings they express are those that you inspire in me.
I haven't gone a day without wanting to tell you.
I would like to see you: that depends on you...
Never doubt, Marie, of my feelings, you would be unfair,
it is a fault that would not suit you well.
A thousand kisses on your hands and
just one on your charming mouth."[10]

In those dark wintry months of February and March, Marie remained in Warsaw isolated from her love, possibly wondering if she would ever again see him, let alone be once more in his arms, in his bed. Her tortured wait would soon come to an end.

---

[9] Napoleon to Josephine, 15 March, 1807, *Foundation Napoléon Archives*

[10] Napoleon to Marie Walewska, 17 March, 1807, *Foundation Napoléon Archives*

Figure 15: Napoleon's East Prussia Field Headquarters: Schloss Finckenstein

Chapter 10: The Castle Finckenstein

"Finally, a castle!" Napoleon was quoted as saying enthusiastically, as he approached the palace, deep in East Prussia, that General Duroc had found for his field headquarters, *Schloss Finckenstein.*

It was in many ways more elegant than the Royal Castle along the Vistula at Warsaw. Situated some fifty miles west of Allenstein and twenty-five miles south of the Baltic Port of Elbląg, *Schloss Finckenstein* reflected the wealth of the excessive profits garnered from that Hanseatic League Port. The castle was built in 1720 as the palatial home of the Prussian Field Marshal, Count Albrecht Konrad Reinhold Fink.

Schloss Finckenstein was located in a village that the Poles called Kamieniec. It had been established in the early 1300s by the Order of Teutonic Knights, the warrior-monks who fought to conquer the pagan forest tribes of the area known as "Prussians." The Knights not only defeated the pagans, but after converting them to Christianity, Germanic secular traders intermarried with them, taking many as their wives. Slowly over the years, the name "Prussians" was transformed to refer to those Germanic peoples who quickly populated the forest regions along the Baltic Sea.

---

[11] History of Finckenstein Castle (original in German) by Christa Mühleisen
Part IV, "Napoleon in Finckenstein"

These Germanized Prussians proved to be aggressive in seizing control over the lands previously held by Poles and other native Baltic Europeans. In 1410, the Polish and Lithuanian armies combined to defeat the Order of the Teutonic Knights in the First Battle of Tannenberg, known to the Poles as the historic Battle of Grunwald. While it was a decisive victory for the two nations that would formally join together well over a century later as a powerful commonwealth, it did not eradicate the Prussians.

After that decisive battle, Kamieniec passed back to Poland and then back again to Prussia. In 1454, the village, along with other lands previously held by the Teutonic Knights, was incorporated as part of Poland by King Casimir IV. In the 18th century, it reverted to becoming part of the joint Kingdom of Brandenburg-Prussia. It would remain there, waiting to adjoin those lands of Poland, which would be stolen late in that century during the First Partition to enlarge their aggressive Prussian state.

Now, after the Battle of Eylau, this region was firmly under Napoleon's control after he had once more driven out the Prussians. From here, Napoleon found it only fitting to direct his final campaign against the Prussian King Friedrich Wilhelm III and his lovely Queen Louise, who were entrapped in Königsberg.

Of course, there was also the young Russian Tsar Alexander and his forces as well, but Napoleon never had any intention of annexing Russia's lands, as he did those of the Prussians. The Emperor did not plan to cross the Niemen River to invade even an acre of Holy Russia. Instead, after defeating the joint Prussian and Russian armies in the War of the Fourth Coalition, Napoleon was confident that Tsar Alexander would accept a peace treaty allowing his Russian army to return to their homeland as devoted allies of the French. In this way, Napoleon envisioned having direct control over most of Europe. In the youthful Tsar, he foresaw having a strong ally against the British to rule over that last, most eastern part of Continental Europe.

In early April 1807, Napoleon took up residence in Castle Finckenstein and quickly sent a protective detail to Warsaw to escort his new mistress, Marie Walewska, to join him there. Marie could not resist the invitation after enduring the torture of being separated from him so abruptly by the Russians' winter incursion.

Marie left her toddler son in Warsaw in the care of her governess, Magdalena Zaczek. She had promised Magdalena that from *Schloss Finckenstein,* she would send back periodic letters, assurances that her son, Marek, was indeed safe and unharmed. Also, she would assure he remained in the Emperor's good graces.

Before another evening penetrated the sullen, gray overcast skies over Kamieniec, Marie found herself once more in the comfort of her lover's arms. They had just satisfied each other's needs, and the moment of union was still fresh between them. Marie decided to fulfill her pledge to Magdalena then and there.

"Napoleon," she bade his attention, finally comfortable calling him by his Christian name after his repeated scolding of her for addressing him as "Sire," "Emperor," or by any other formal title.

"Yes, my love," he responded.

"Will you do me a great favor?"

"If it is possible that within the capabilities that I possess as Emperor of the French that I may, then, of course, my lovely, I will…" he teased, "…what is this tremendous request, my dear?"

"I have a governess in Warsaw who looks after my son while I am away with you. She has been in my service since before I was married."

"Oh, for such a tremendous length of time?" he jested. "What was that, two and a half years ago? Even before I was crowned Emperor?"

"Don't mock me," Marie said, swatting her open palm against his chest. "I am most serious."

"So you are! You have a governess. She needs what, my sweet? A title? How about the Princess of Poznań? Perhaps the Duchess of Danzig? We will have to drive the Prussians out of that Baltic port first, I'm afraid, but that will come to pass soon enough. You'll be pleased to know that I have my best Pole, General Dąbrowski, assisting Marshal Lefebvre on its planning even now."

Marie pulled him closer and reached up to take his face into her palms. Leaning forward, she kissed him on his lips.

"Why do you enjoy mocking me so?" she said, "My governess, Magdalena, is herself a mother. Her son fights for you. He fights for both Poland and France, but most devotedly, he fights for his Emperor. Magdalena only wishes to know that he is safe. She only wishes to know that he lives, that he is unharmed."

"Who is this miscreant soldier who does not even write his own mother regularly? Even as busy as I am as Emperor, I still steal away a few minutes to devotedly write to my own mother. Now, must I be burdened with the labor of informing another man's mother of his health also?"

"You need do nothing, my love. Only tell me of this soldier's condition, and I will relay his status to her. She worries so much for her son."

"You expect me to know the health of every Pole who raises a sabre or a lance for the Empire of France. Who is this man-child who cannot even behave like a proper gentleman?"

"He is one you know very well, my love," Marie coaxed him. "Magdalena's son is none other than the *Capitaine* of the Polish Lancers, Marek Zaczek."

"Ah, Marek Zaczek!" Napoleon said in mock surprise. "Zaczek is no child. He is a man's man, a soldier's soldier. Possibly, he is the best horseman riding in all the cavalry of the Empire. But if he cannot find a few idle moments to write to his own mother, well, my love, I will remedy that."

"No, darling, you won't," Marie said. "There is bad blood between them. I do not understand exactly why, but I only wish to inform her occasionally of her son's safety. If you will have General Duroc keep me apprised of his status, then there is nothing else for you personally to do. Nothing would please me more, my darling, to make my Magdalena happy in that way! After all, without her, I could not be here with you!"

"Then, my love, you must tell her that this day he is not only safe and protecting me here at Finckenstein, but that during the Battle of Eylau, he was among the Imperial Guard who saved me from the clutches of the Russians. I was in an observation tower, the spire of a church, when the hill it stood on was overrun, and had it not been for Zaczek and others, I would most likely be in Königsberg or Saint Petersburg in prison this very night. Zaczek is, perhaps, only second to Dąbrowski himself, the Pole most near to my own heart. He has been since he came to me from the Austrians on the bridge at Lodi a decade ago. What a sight that was, his rescuing my panicked white steed under such heavy fire. He was the very image of bravery in action. Yes, tell your Magdalena her son is safe and secure in my affections."

"Thank you, my love," Marie said. "In the future, every time we lie here and you tell me he is safe, it will be another stitch sewing my heart ever more closely to your own."

"My beautiful Polish delight," he said, "my heart is already so deeply immersed in yours. I will tell you what I can of Zaczek, but know that I already count your heart among my most prized possessions. I will have Duroc report to you regularly when I myself am elsewhere distracted by my imperial responsibilities."

"Then I will now press my last request," Marie said. "Do not leave me to pursue the Russians again. Allow your marshals to wage the war you plan from the safety of this castle. You did not have to tell me you were nearly captured at Eylau. My deepest fear is that, against your will, you might be taken away from me."

"My dear," Napoleon exclaimed, "would you ask a lion not to roar! An eagle not to soar! A tiger not to stalk its prey!"

"But Napoleon," Marie cried, tears streaming from her face as she envisioned him lying dead on a battlefield, "you are such a target for every enemy soldier of the Empire. Each one would be proud to boast it was he who shot you dead, a boast that would pierce my very heart. I could never afford to lose you, my love."

Napoleon scoffed at this. "Instead, you would kill me slowly by imprisoning me in a garden of roses? Away from the battles, for which I live?" He grasped the corner of the bedsheets and gently dabbed the tears from her cheeks. A wry smile creased his face.

"Do not worry your pretty little head, *mon cherie,*" the Emperor retorted, "because for every enemy combatant that would love to take my life, I have a thousand Marek Zaczek's willing to give their last breath to protect me. And I have a little secret for you, darling."

"Tell me, my Napoleon," Marie said, no longer crying, but her face still streaked with tears. By then, she merely sniffled like a small child. "What is this secret?"

"No, it is too soon," he replied, "you must wait a bit longer. After all, it will be my guarantee that you stay here with me." He laughed as he wiped away the tears that clung to her face.

"Stay with you? My Napoleon, you will never shed me again. No, I will come with you to the ends of the earth, my Emperor!" she said with a coquettish smile, her tear-drenched eyes once again beaming through their wash.

"You have no idea how it pleases me to hear your words, my love," Napoleon replied, "but this secret is one that will please you and your countrymen very much. You will have to wait just a few days more, until that devil in his diplomat's clothes, my Minister Talleyrand, arrives here at Finckenstein."

"Monsieur Talleyrand? Do I get to meet him?"

"Of course, my lovely Marie. Monsieur Talleyrand carries your surprise with him. Soon enough, he will arrive, and it will please you, I am sure."

"My Emperor," Marie said, her eyes clear but still damp, "It is you alone who pleases me so! Can you not see this?"

These words were shared in the time when Marek's battalion of Polish Lancers was being expanded significantly to a full regiment consisting of four such squadrons. The Emperor had for some time prized this country's fighting cavalry, ever since they had first fought as Dąbrowski's Legions in Italy. The Honor Guard of aristocrats' sons, which the Emperor was given upon entering Poland, had impressed him all the more. He decided then to expand the Lancers. This was to be his gift for the Countess.

Talleyrand brought with him the *"Ordre de Bataille,"* or Commissioning Order, for the Polish Lancer Regiment. In it, Article 4 required the new regiment to retain *"four sub-adjutant-majors from among the Poles, who formerly were on duty in the Legions in France, one standard-bearer, and four surgeons…"*

With the Empire taking control of the Polish lands, nearly every Polish nobleman wanted either himself or his sons to ride as a member of the newly expanded Polish Lancers. Article 5 set the standard as: *"To be enlisted into the Chevaux-légers Corps one has to be a landowner or the son of a landowner, be more than 18 years old, and less than 40, and come with his own horse, uniform, caparison and other equipment according to the regulations…"*

One would think that this expansion of the Polish Lancers would have been welcomed by Marek. But it came at a terrible cost to his self-confidence. In order to appease the noblemen of his country, the leadership of this regiment would be taken out of the grasp of Marek and transferred to one of their own. For while Marek was proudly counted by them as being Polish, he was not a nobleman in any sense of his countrymen's minds.

So, in deference to the desires of the Polish aristocrats, Count Wincenty Krasiński was named as the regimental commander and the unit's Colonel. After all, these nobles would be entrusting the lives of their sons to this nobleman's command. Still, this came as a hard slap in the face to Marek Zaczek, who himself had served in Dąbrowski's Legions and fought alongside the Emperor in many of his most significant and most successful battles. Despite his demonstrated skill and experience, he now would report to a regimental colonel a full ten years younger than himself, and with no real experience at that point in battle.

Instead, Marek was promoted to Lieutenant Colonel as the second in command to Count Krasiński. This position was not even described in the Commissioning Order, but no one was eager to bring that fact to the Emperor's attention. They merely saw it for what it was - a reward for Zaczek's dedication to Napoleon in the many battles against Austria, Prussia, and Russia. In this role, Marek was given the responsibility for selecting the horsemen from Dąbrowski's Legions to meet the requirements of Article 4.

Marek first selected the four *capitaines*, the squadron Commanding Officers: Tomasz Łubieński, Ferdynand Stokowski, Jan Kozietulski, and Henryk Kamieński. Each man had ridden bravely under Marek when he was *capitaine,* and they all had his full confidence. Marek was sure that these men would capably lead each of the newly formed squadrons of the expanded regiment.

Marek next selected as his own personal staff four other men who had ridden alongside him in battle for many years. First, there were the two brothers Antoni and Edziu Pilarczyk. Antoni was the more stalwart of the two, the elder brother with a head for organizational detail. Marek would lean on him as his *de facto* chief of staff. His brother Edziu was more of a gambler and a truly free spirit, but no one Marek had ever ridden into battle with had fought with more ferocity and tenacity. The two brothers would quarrel often with each other, but Marek had grown used to that.

Next, Marek added perhaps his oldest friend. His name was Mieczysław Wieczorek, and he had already been in Dąbrowski's Legions when Marek had defected on that bridge at Lodi over a decade ago. True to his name (for *Mieczysław Wieczorek* can be translated to *"glorious sabre fast as the wind"* in Polish), he was the finest swordsman Marek had ever encountered. His feints and bluffs would confuse and frustrate an enemy until his lethal parry stroke was thrust. It was he who had taught Marek how to handle a sabre after his defection, and this education had served him well many times in battle. Marek felt he owed Mieczysław his career, for it was his friend who had made him a true cavalier.

The last of Marek's staff was rounded out by a half-Polish, half-Persian newcomer to the cavalry, Klęczeć Sałeh. He had been added by Napoleon himself, in the throes of completing a peace accord with the Shah of Persia, whose delegation had already arrived at *Schloss Finckenstein*. Marek had tried to gain the release of his friend Rydek of Toruń from Marshal Bernadotte for this final spot, but to no avail. The Emperor demanded that the half-Persian Klęczeć Sałeh be appointed to impress the Shah's visiting delegation. Thus, that final position was given to the procedurally fanatical and highly competent Sałeh, even though he was neither half the horseman nor fighter that Rydek had proven himself to be.

In April of 1807, after weeks of training under Colonel Krasiński, the raw recruits were presented as a regiment to the Emperor. The result was an absolute nightmare. The simplest marching and parade orders were poorly executed. Horsemen awkwardly bumped into one another, and the entire review became a debacle. Napoleon was livid and was quoted as having said,

"Do these Poles not understand anything in being a soldier? But, oh, how they fight!"[12]

---

[12] Napoleon's Elite Cavalry, Text by Edward Ryan, Paintings by Lucien Rousselot, Greenhill Books, 1999

Colonel Krasiński's initial mistake was his refusal to turn the training of the raw recruits over to Marek Zaczek and his staff. These soldiers (all except for Sałeh) had led the Lancers for many years, earning the Emperor's most profound respect. Instead, Krasiński relied on other newly recruited sons of aristocrats whom he knew and had ridden alongside for years. He attempted to train the raw recruits with these men, although none had ever before ridden for the Empire, let alone fought for it or offered up their lives in battle. The result was a disaster witnessed by the Emperor.

"Have these men," Napoleon abraded Krasiński, "not been with me since Dąbrowski's Legions conquered Italy alongside the French at my command? Why do you think I explicitly called out their inclusion in this regiment? For you to ignore their discipline? To render supine the way they know in their bones how to fight? You will use Marek Zaczek and his delegates to train these recruits, Count Krasiński, or I will quickly find another Colonel Regimental Commander from among your countrymen."

After this debacle, the responsibility of the regimental training was returned to Marek and his staff. Horsemanship was taught by Marek, swordplay by Mieczysław Wieczorek, battle strategy by Antoni Pilarczyk, and guerrilla tactics by his younger brother Edziu. Parade etiquette was left to the half-Persian Klęczeć Sałeh, who quickly mastered its intricacies.

The first decision made by this cadre of trainers was a difficult one. After quadrupling the number of lancers, it became apparent that mastery of their most highly prized weapon, the lance, that instrument which had given them their proud name, must wait until other, more foundational skills of the expanded unit were mastered. The regiment's use of the lance in battle must be deferred until they could master more conventional armaments.

So, the unit would be officially known as the Polish Light Cavalry Regiment of the Imperial Guard for the immediate future. Until their traditional weapon could be mastered again, they would no longer be known as the *Polish Lancers of La Grande Armée.*

On the fourth of May, Napoleon signed the Treaty of Finckenstein with the Shah of Persia, who had been at war with Russia since the previous December. After that point, Marek considered the release of the half-Persian Klęczeć Sałeh, hoping to replace him with his friend Rydek of Toruń. However, by then, Marek had become most impressed with Sałeh's adherence to detail, especially in protocol and procedures. He decided the man had earned his keep, so no request was made to replace him.

It took a few months, but the efforts of Marek's staff paid handsome dividends. By early June, Marek had drilled the units tirelessly until he assessed that all four squadrons of his expanded regiment were functioning nearly as efficiently as his older, singular battalion. All except the mastery of the lance, that is. That weapon remained outside their level of skill.

Of course, these recruits had not yet been battle-tested as had his original battalion of lancers, which had fought ever so valiantly at Jena and Austerlitz. Still, Marek realized the lessons of battle could only be learned by the scars of experience.

Marek knew that conflict itself was the great separator, for only the trials of battle would sieve out those on horseback with valiant hearts from others who would freeze with fear amid the strains and pressures of committing a mistake that could cost them their lives. Only upon being exposed to the rigors of a most mortal hostility could the bravest soldiers be selected from those who would hesitate in battle, and put all others at risk.

The one area of the regiment over which Marek had no authority was the assignment of the regimental surgeons. The *Grande Armée*'s Surgeon-in-Chief, the Baron Dominique Jean Larrey, selected these. Dr. Larrey had first served with Napoleon at Toulon, quickly became the Surgeon-in-Chief of France's Revolutionary Armies in Italy, and even joined Napoleon's Expedition to Egypt. He had introduced many advanced concepts into the *Grande Armée*, including the forerunners of triage and field ambulances.

Dr. Larrey was assigned the task of selecting three regimental surgeons for the new Regiment of Polish Light Cavalry. The first two were selected completely on the basis of competence, but the last, a mere lowly third-class position, was awarded to a raw medical recruit named Judasz Zdrajca. He was assigned at the behest of a Polish nobleman from the area near the border with the Austrian province of Galicia. This particular third-class surgeon, Judasz Zdrajca, would ultimately play a most significant role in the life to come of Lieutenant Colonel Marek Zaczek.

Chapter 11: Sowing The Seeds of Deception

arsaw was still reverberating with the energy of the Emperor and his *Grande Armée*, even though they were commanded out of the East Prussian headquarters at *Schloss Finckenstein* by then. All Poles anxiously awaited the battle that would finally defeat the Russians and Prussians once and for all. Then, they surmised, they were sure to have their homeland returned to them. To that end, rumors of Countess Marie Walewska's tryst with the Emperor circulated wildly, often with the inference that she was enjoying her *"mission to revive her country's sovereignty,"* perhaps a bit too much.

Of course, Magdalena knew the full measure of the truth but would never confirm it to any other soul except her daughter-in-law, Maya. She also would never comment on it to her sister-in-law, Ewelina. That last conversation was not too difficult to avoid, for Ewelina had taken to leaving the town home as much as possible now that the winter weather had finally broken. She would depart for morning mass and not return until well after dark.

"So, Maya," Magdalena said after reading her latest letter from Marie Walewska at *Schloss Finckenstein,* "Countess Marie writes that Marek has done well in training the light horse regiment over the past several weeks. The Emperor is gaining such confidence that he feels they will soon be ready to fight in their full number. Only a select few were chosen to fight at Eylau, but Marek has now readied the rest for battle. Countess Marie also writes that our Marek remains healthy and safe."

"Praise be to Jesus Christ," Maya said thankfully, "but it also surely means Marek will lead them into battle when that time comes. That is what perhaps scares me the most. You know he was never one to shy away from danger. I am so thankful that you are receiving these reports from the Countess, as I worry so much about him, but why does Marek refuse to write to us on his own?"

"Because my son is very headstrong, I presume," Magdalena said. "You have known him nearly as long as I have, Maya, ever since you were born. That, after all, was only a couple of years after I gave birth to him at the *folwark* in Wieliczka."

"Yes," Maya agreed, "but no one knows a child as deeply or as well as the woman who bore him…"

"…Until he grows to be a man when his wife replaces her in his heart," Magdalena sighed.

"I feel," Maya replied, 'that through all the years that we knew each other, I only possessed his heart on two occasions after leaving the *folwark* - during the weeks we shared in Paris when we conceived Czesław and in the more recent days when I first presented him with that same son. Yet, whether I have his heart any longer or not, I know that when he puts his mind to something, his will becomes immovable. Still, I wish he would not harbor such animosity against you or myself. Neither of our situations is of our own making, are they? Why can't he accept this?"

"You might as well ask God, *'Why does the wind blow?'* to get a faster reply than waiting for Marek to accept our plight." Magdalena then looked around the room, searching for the one she wished not to hear her comments. Having confirmed her sister-in-law was absent, she said, "Ewelina can be just as stubborn as Marek. She cannot shed the grief of losing her husband, Jacek, and their twin sons. She blames everything on my Marek. I regret ever sharing with her the dark secret of his birth. Alas, I was but a child then and needed her assistance. Now she harbors such resentment against us both. I fear what venom brews within her."

"It has not even been six months since her dreadful losses," Maya argued, "give Ewelina more time. She will one day realize how good you have been to her all these years. Soon enough, the scales of contempt will fall from her eyes. She will return to you."

"But you do not fully understand," Magdalena said, "her contempt began not only with the death of these three, but over ten years earlier when they were taken along with Marek into the Austrian army. She is certain that your father, the Duke, sent them all off to war only as an excuse to separate Marek from yourself. In that way, she blames Marek for having taken away her three men, her entire family. She likely blames you as much as she does me in her demented logic."

"And that is why she refuses to stay here with us?" Maya asked. "Day after day, she leaves at dawn and returns only at dusk, or even later under the darkness of night."

"Where on earth does she go?" Magdalena asked aloud. "It is as if she hides all day in the devil's shadow. Oh, how she worries me. She has too much time to think about how she will take her revenge. And every day it is not taken, her vile mind only sharpens the details of how it will be so punishingly delivered one day when we least expect it."

"Let us hope that day never comes. Give her time," Maya repeated. "Pray to Jesus and the Blessed Virgin to soften Ewelina's embittered heart, especially during the coming Virgin's month of May. I do so each and every day, when I also pray to her to ask the Almighty to thaw Marek's frozen heart. The Holy Mother will hear our prayers and intercede for us. I know she will."

"My only prayer is that the piety of your blind faith is richly rewarded, my child," Magdalena conceded.

That very day in Warsaw, Ewelina met secretly with an older man in an apartment in the Praga district, just across the Vistula. The accommodations were modest but clean, and the man was every bit the gentleman one might presume him to be by his dress. He wore a long gray overcoat, striped trousers, and a fine white dress shirt. His gray hair was well barbered, as was his beard, neat and trim.

In fact, Ewelina had been meeting with him off and on for several weeks. So much so, that many of the neighbors cast her accusing glances when she would walk up to the building. Yet there was nothing "unseemly" about the relationship between the gentleman and herself. No, their relationship, although it was kept in utmost secrecy, was professional. She was his patient. He professed to be her doctor.

"Dr. Olszewski," Ewelina said that day, "has the Count rendered a decision on my request to return."

"I am afraid, my dear," the doctor replied, "Count Von Arndt has been quite occupied with the coming spring needs of his *folwark*. In addition, there is still the matter of your being a resident of Prussia, as is your sister-in-law, Magdalena."

"Yes, but the Emperor is here now," Ewelina said. "I know the entirety of Prussian Poland assumes Napoleon will annex us as a sovereign state again under his Empire soon enough. And as the French Empire and the Austrians are at peace, there should be no problem in my returning to Wieliczka, should there be?"

"In theory, no," the doctor said, "but there are many assumptions in your statement. First, it assumes the Tsar will not overcome and drive out the French and revert control once more to their allies, the Prussians. Also, it assumes that the two empires of Austria and France will remain at peace, which we have seen can always shift dramatically back toward the hellfire of war. "

"But did you relay to the Count how earnestly I wish to serve him on the *folwark* again? I am old, it is true, but I have much energy left in my bones."

"Dear Ewelina," Doctor Olszewski said, "I would hardly think of you as old. You are not even yet well into your fifties. You appear to be in excellent health, at least physically. The medicines I have given to you should help you with your state of mind. But do not worry yourself, I will continue to advocate on your behalf with the Count. I am sure in time, he will come to welcome you home again. But, I think you may need to prepare yourself…"

"For what, exactly, my Doctor?" Ewelina asked.

"…for the Count to ask you for a demonstration of loyalty. He is a man who provides well for those dedicated to his service. I stand as an excellent example of his generosity, of his patronage to those who are loyal to him and his causes."

"But, good Doctor," she answered, "assure he knows that I will do whatever he needs me to do on his behalf. Please tell Count Von Arndt that I will serve him in any way I can. I just wish to spend the later years of my lonely life on the *folwark* where I was born and raised. His *folwark* at Wieliczka. I need to get as far from my sister-in-law Magdalena and her son Marek, for between the two of them, they have provided me only a life of great suffering."

"Don't worry, my child," Doctor Olszewski said to her, "You will be rid of her and her son, I assure you. Now the hour is late, and I must rest for tomorrow, I have an early appointment before I head back to Galicia. I will meet you here again in two weeks' time."

"Yes," Ewelina said, "with a decision from the Count?"

"Hopefully," he said cautiously. "Hopefully, I will bring good news for you from the Count."

"Please thank the Count once more for recovering the bodies of my sons at Austerlitz and for giving them such a proper burial at the cemetery in Wieliczka."

"Yes, yes," he said impatiently, "I have many times already, and I will once more. And for your husband's remains as well."

"You assured me that Jacek is buried far from my boys," she pleaded, "please tell me he is not buried near them. The man fired them with the Emperor's cannons and most likely killed our sons. He took his own life like a coward rather than face me. His corpse should not be buried in the same cemetery as theirs."

"As I have said many times before," Olszewski explained, "his grave is on the distant other side of the *folwark*. Your sons are Austrian war heroes and deserve to be buried with dignity in the cemetery. Your husband was not only a suicide but, even if only briefly, a veteran of Austria's enemy, *La Grande Armée*. Both reasons preclude his being interred in the *folwark* cemetery. When you come home to stay, I will show you the location of his unmarked grave. Now I must really insist you go, my dear. Until two weeks' time, *do widzenia.*"

Ewelina left the doctor in his rented Praga apartment and walked the streets of Warsaw, her spirits buoyed by the hope the good doctor had imparted within her. In the pocket of her ragged, shabby coat was a bottle of laudanum, enough to last her two weeks, although she knew it would be gone in half that time. That was if she could control herself to make it last even that long.

The next morning, the doctor from Wieliczka kept his appointment with a young man in the *stare miasto,* Warsaw's old town. The doctor was dressed as he had been the day before, but the younger man he met that morning was dressed out in a brand new uniform of the First Polish Light Horse Regiment.

"Count Von Arndt asked me to relay to you exactly how proud he is of your being assigned to the new Polish Regiment in Napoleon's *Grande Armée*," Doctor Olszewski said.

"Please thank the Count on my behalf for his efforts in making that become a reality," the third-class surgeon Judasz Zdrajca said. "I am unsure how an Austrian Count has such influence with the *Grande Armée*, but thank him on my behalf, *Dziadek.*"

"I will, my grandson," said Doctor Olszewski. "The Count merely asked me which Polish aristocrats to get to plead your case, and the rest took care of itself."

He did not mention the significant bribes that he himself had to carry across the border to secure those aristocrats' pleadings. While not a single *złoty* found its way into Chief Surgeon, Dr. Larrey's pockets, the money nonetheless sweetened the aristocrats' tongues that whispered into his ears.

"Well, *Dziadek,* thank you also," his grandson said.

"Look at you," Doctor Olszewski said. "You look so splendid in that uniform. A field surgeon no less. You make me so proud. But, I must tell you that the time may come when the Austrian Count may call on you for a small favor. Don't worry, nothing treasonous. Just a little information every now and then."

"Of course, *Dziadek,* of course," his grandson Judasz Zdrajca replied with a sly smile. "Just no battle plans, or the movements of our troops." He laughed as he said the last line, attempting to dress his serious concern in the disguise of a joke.

"Of course not," Doctor Olszewski said, "I would never allow even Count Von Arndt to put my grandson in such a tenuous position."

Chapter 12: The Retribution of Count Maximilian Von Arndt

The Austrian Count Maximilian Von Arndt had long ago set a plan into play to obtain the riches from both the Wieliczka and Bochnia salt mines in the Austrian territory of Galicia, made up of the partitioned Polish lands. Von Arndt had been sent by the Austrian Emperor as overseer when both mines were under the control of Duke Cyprian Sdanowicz, Maya's father. The Count initiated a series of events that would strip the two lucrative mines away from the Duke and bring them under his own control.

Von Arndt discovered that the Bochnia mine had once legitimately been the property of Magdalena's parents, a rival duke and his wife, before both were deported to Russia at the behest of Duke Sdanowicz. Their daughter had been taken onto Sdanowicz's *folwark* as the peasant, Magda. Having discovered this deceit, Von Arndt pleaded Magda's case before the Austrian Emperor, resulting in the Bochnia mine being stripped away from the Duke and becoming her property. The Austrian Emperor's Court also reinstated Magdalena as the Duchess she had been at birth. When the Wieliczka mine was ordered stripped away from the Duke as punishment for his misdeeds, it was awarded to Count Von Arndt.

The final part of Count Von Arndt's avarice was that which failed him. He planned to marry the Duchess Magdalena and thus, through marriage, consolidate both mines under his direct control.

He was well on his way to doing so, when the woman's son, Marek, defected from the Austrian infantry to the French by crossing the bridge at Lodi in Northern Italy in May of 1796.

As for Magdalena, the Count had truly long been enamored with her beauty and had favored her greatly. He sought her company out every time he visited the *folwark,* but it had always been jealously denied him by the Duke. However, once Sdanowicz was out of the way, her son Marek spoiled everything by defecting.

Count Von Arndt was outraged. He could no longer remain in good standing with the Emperor's Court at Vienna if he were to marry the mother of a defector. So the planned marriage was called off. Thus, the Count's deception to consolidate the two mines under his control was foiled. So, instead, he discredited the reinstated Duchess at the Viennese court, which ultimately resulted in her being stripped of both the Bochnia mine and her title.

Count Von Arndt then planned to lure the defrocked Duchess out of Kraków and imprison her upon his *folwark* at Wieliczka. Just before Magdalena could be apprehended by luring her south across the Vistula River bridge, she became suspicious and fled north to Warsaw, leaving all her possessions behind and arriving in the capital near penniless.

The Austrian Emperor caught wind of the Count's ruse to abduct the woman, and as a result, the Bochnia mine that was to go to him was instead awarded to another nobleman. The progression of events denied Von Arndt a lucrative stream of revenue. However, even without the second property, control of the Wieliczka mine alone still made him very wealthy.

This chain of events had discredited him with the Royal Court at Vienna. This enraged the Count, who became transfixed on gaining vengeance on Magdalena. Despite his many advances over the years, she had never given herself to him, not even when they were betrothed. He swore he would one day take her by force and in doing so, have his revenge upon her and also her son Marek.

Years later, the Count could not believe his good graces when he was informed that the bodies of the twin sons of the woman Ewelina had been recovered from the lakes at Austerlitz. Of course, it had been his doing all along that her sons, along with her husband, were ever conscripted into the Austrian army at all. Von Arndt paid dearly to have both boys' bodies recovered and returned to Wieliczka for burial in the *folwark* cemetery.

Von Arndt considered this to be an investment, knowing it would drive a wedge between the boys' peasant mother, Ewelina, and her sister-in-law, Magdalena. What he did not foresee was that in the tempest of that crucible he had forged, the boys' father would also take his own life, increasing the calamity of the situation. Still, even this would work to his advantage in manipulating the peasant Ewelina to do his bidding.

Count Von Arndt used the burial of the father and his two sons as a sledge hammer to drive deep the spike of his revenge. He leveraged his *folwark's* physician, Dr. Olszewski, a well-respected individual long known to Ewelina, to begin a string of meetings with the bereaved woman to stoke her anger. He also ordered Dr. Olszewski to lace the woman's grief with laudanum and to continue doing so until he directed otherwise.

Then, the final stake in the tent was to bribe the Polish aristocrats so that Dr. Olszewski's own grandson, Judasz Zdrajca would be named as a field surgeon, third-class, in the newly formed Regiment of Polish Light Cavalry in *La Grande Armée*. This being done, Von Arndt would then wield like pincers the grief of Ewelina and the implanted surgeon to crush Marek Zaczek and gain his revenge on Magdalena. Von Arndt was outraged that the two of them had disrupted his plans and, in doing so, had cut the size of his fortune by half. Now that Austria and France were no longer engaged in active warfare, and Marek Zaczek was in Poland fighting for Napoleon, Count Maximilian Von Arndt would employ deceit and trickery to make the most of his retribution.

His plan was simple: to use the doctor's grandson to keep track of Marek's status. When it would be most believable, Magdalena's son would be declared seriously wounded in battle. Von Arndt knew he could use the grief of such a moment to then lure Magdalena into the territory of Austria on the premise of attending to her son. As soon as she came onto Austrian soil, he would have her secretly abducted and brought to Wieliczka. Once there, the Count would retain her as his captive, albeit unwilling, concubine.

To ensure his plan would be effective, he had Doctor Olszewski string along the woman's sister-in-law, Ewelina, who desperately wanted to cleave herself from Magdalena's household and return to the *folwark*. Count Von Arndt would play Ewelina so that she would become an unwitting accomplice in his deceit.

Chapter 13: A Great Compromise: The Grand Duchy of Warsaw

Napoleon found himself trapped. While he planned the military defeat of his army's last real threat left in all of Continental Europe, the Russians, he was at a quandary as to how to solve the Polish Question, as it was called. He could militarily defeat the Tsar's armies, but had no intention of invading the Russian lands. Instead, he would negotiate a peace treaty from a position of strength but with outright respect for the youthful Tsar Alexander. In defeat, he would offer to make Russia his ally, while he severely punished the Prussians who had so audaciously dared to press their crumbling war machine against the French.

But what was to be done with Poland? It had been swallowed whole not only by the Russians and the Prussians in the last decades of the previous century, but also by the Austrians. If he attempted to reinstate the country in full, as he had for so long led the Poles to believe he would, both Russia and Austria would most likely be incensed to the point of waging further war. That was unacceptable, as Napoleon needed urgently to return to Paris after his lengthy campaign. He and his *Grande Armée* had been gone far too long from France. Reinstating the country of Poland was, at that time, out of the question altogether, for he would face revolt from within the ranks of his troops if he were to reignite war with both the Russians and the Austrians instead of returning to France.

Even to award the Poles with only the lands taken from Prussia, if they were reinstated under the name of Poland, it would only encourage the Poles to seek repatriation of the remaining lands taken during the Partitions by Austria and Russia. This was completely unacceptable to the Emperor.

The Prussians held no sway in Napoleon's concerns. Had it not been for the Tsar's army, they would already have been crushed. No, once Bennigsen was defeated, Napoleon knew what he would do. He would allow Russia and Austria to keep the lands they had taken from Poland during the Partitions, but not the Prussians. He would return those lands to the Poles in the form of a new, limited province to be called "the Duchy of Warsaw."

The Emperor would have it administered by Prince Jozef Poniatowski, nephew of the last reigning king of Poland, but the Duchy would not in itself be sovereign. After all, Napoleon was not sure the Poles had the political acumen to govern themselves. Had they not made such a frivolous mess of that during the Partitions?

Instead, the Duchy of Warsaw would come under the control of the King of Saxony, whom Napoleon needed to favor. As the Saxons were the close neighbors of the Prussians, they had kept watch on France's enemy for some time. So the Saxon King, Frederick Augustus, would be rewarded by ruling over the Grand Duchy, with the Polish Prince Poniatowski running its daily affairs.

By carving out this new political entity, the Poles would have to be satisfied with their limited gains, taken from the spoils of the Prussians, who, by the Emperor's estimate, would lose nearly a third of their empire to the Grand Duchy of Warsaw. The Poles would have a reinstated, Polish-speaking, Polish-administered territory. While it was true that it would not be a sovereign state, it would make up roughly a third of what the country had once been. That should be enough to keep the Polish soldiers fighting on the Empire's behalf in future wars. And he had seen firsthand over a decade just how hard these Poles could fight!

Napoleon had sent to Berlin to have his Minister Talleyrand join him at *Schloss Finckenstein*. Upon his arrival, a discreet meeting was held in Napoleon's apartment with the French Minister and Countess Marie Walewska.

The quarters were spacious, consisting of two adjacent apartments looking out upon the formal gardens of the estate. In this way, Marie and Napoleon enjoyed privacy, to as much of a degree as the ever-protective turbaned Mameluke manservant, Roustam, could provide. Their safety was assured as well by a protective unit of Imperial Guard encamped at the other end of the expansive gardens.

The parlor of Napoleon's apartment was covered in fresh-cut flowers, as was that of Countess Marie. It was as if Roustam was attempting to compete with the colors and delicate scents of the garden outside their doors. Minister Talleyrand hobbled in, leaning heavily on his walking stick, and stood before Napoleon's beautiful mistress.

"Monsieur First Minister," Napoleon began, "it is my delight to introduce you to the most lovely of all Polish aristocrats, the Countess Marie Walewska."

Talleyrand bowed at the waist before her, then took her hand to his mouth and kissed it respectfully.

"Countess," Napoleon next introduced his minister, "I am pleased to present you to the Prince de Bénévent, the Minister of the Empire, Monsieur Charles-Maurice de Talleyrand-Perigord."

Marie curtseyed before him, saying, "Your Serene Highness, what an honor it is to finally meet you. I feel as if I already have, as the Emperor speaks of you so often."

"Madame Countess," Talleyrand replied, "I assure you the honor and pleasure are all mine. Do not allow the Emperor's words to stand for me any longer, for I now stand before you as a mere humble servant of the Empire."

"Serene? Humble? *Eh?*" Napoleon rolled his eyes and muttered loud enough to be heard, "These are but the flattering words of diplomacy! Outside that, they are but mere lies."

"Perhaps, Sire, perhaps," Talleyrand mused, "but the undeniable truth of this occasion is the beauty of Madame! A rare flower indeed."

Talleyrand's words seemed only to irritate the Emperor further, for he knew the Minister to be nothing of a gentleman in his pursuit of the feminine wares.

After the introductions were completed and all were seated at table, Minister Talleyrand presented the announcement of the new Polish Light Horse Regiment, and discussed each article point by point with the Countess.

"Magdalena, my governess, will be so delighted," Marie said as he finished. She saw the puzzled look on the minister's face before she added, "Magdalena is the mother of *Capitaine* Marek Zaczek. I assume this will mean a promotion for her son to lead this new regiment?"

Talleyrand looked to the Emperor, whose hand gesture indicated that he should go on and explain.

"Countess," the minister began, "diplomacy, much like yourself, is a fragile and delicate entity. Often, some sacrifices are made to assure its protection. In this case, you are correct that *Capitaine* Zaczek will be promoted to Lieutenant Colonel, in fact. But, in order to assure that we remain in the good graces of your country's leadership, Lieutenant Colonel Zaczek will not lead this regiment. That position will go to Colonel Krasiński, and Zaczek will be his adjutant officer. In this way, the aristocrats of Warsaw can be sure the regiment is to be led by one of their own sons…"

"…And not by the mere offspring of one of their governesses," Marie finished his sentence in a dejected tone.

"That is a very astute way to put the matter, Madame," Talleyrand conceded.

"But *Capitaine* Zaczek does not even meet these requirements, as he is not the son of a landowner," she continued to contest. "The declaration does not even have a position called out as a Lieutenant Colonel. Are you assuring me that he will be retained as such?"

Napoleon felt it necessary to intercede. "*Mon amie,* I, your Emperor, assure you that Magdalena's son will always be with this unit so long as he is fit for service to the Empire. The man has the heart of a lion, and the skill on horseback of any Dragoon, Cuirassier, or Cavalier of the Empire. I, as Emperor, have the prerogative to add any position I like to these announcements, or waive any requirements I see fit. No, I assure you, my love, your Magdalena's Marek will be the shadow of Colonel Krasiński in leading this regiment of excellent Polish horsemen."

"Thank you, Sire," she replied stiffly, not wishing to use the Emperor's given name in front of the minister. "You have allayed my concerns. Yet, I do have another question. What is this term referring to regarding Prince Poniatowski?"

Her question prompted another discomforting glance by Talleyrand to Napoleon, who again waved him on to explain.

"Madame Countess," the minister began, "you, of course, refer to Article 9, which states that all recruits are instructed to:

...*present themselves to Prince Poniatowski, director of the Department of War of the Duchy of Warsaw.*"[13]

"Yes," she replied, "I am not familiar with that last reference in the prince's title. What is this Duchy of Warsaw?"

------

[13] *Ordre de Bataille, First Light Cavalry Lancer Regiment of the Imperial Guard (Polish), Imperial Communication of La Grande Armée, April 6th, 1807*

"My beautiful darling Marie," Napoleon raised a hand to Talleyrand, indicating that he had changed his mind and would explain to her, "often diplomacy, like life itself, is confusing and revealed only in layers. Soon, I will unveil the fullness of my generous gift to you, *mais non,* my gift to your entire country."

"Another gift?" she asked, "and for my entire country?"

"Yes, but I will explain that to you in a few days' time," he said. "For now, trust in your Emperor to have your country's best interests in mind at all times. Now, Minister Talleyrand and I have other matters to attend to. Please forgive me for keeping you in suspense for but a little bit longer."

With these words, the meeting was over. Another rush of pleasantries exuded from the minister. Marie could only think of all the derogatory comments Napoleon had made regarding him, especially how Talleyrand was known to go through many women wherever he traveled. Throughout their meeting, Marie felt the probing measure of the minister's gaze on her and thought she sensed in Napoleon a streak of jealousy. Had the Emperor not such need for Talleyrand's diplomatic entreaties, like the one they were engaged in with the Shah of Persia at that time, Marie was certain her love would have dismissed the minister there and then.

A few days later, Marie awoke in the Emperor's bed to an unusual beam of diffused sunlight flooding in through the curtains. For the first time since her arrival, the canopy of gray clouds had parted and the blue skies of April peered down from beyond them.

"How I wish all this business of war and battles were but memories of a dream," she said softly aloud to herself.

"But my darling," Napoleon startled her, thinking him to still be asleep, "it is exactly that business that was responsible for bringing me to you."

"My love," she replied, "if only I had met you in Paris, how grand life would be with you there."

"Mais mon cherie," he said, "life can be no more perfect than this very moment we share together. Ah, my gift to you…"

Marie's face sparkled elegantly in the glow of the *lumière du soleil tôt le matin.* Her cheeks had a radiant glow fueled by true contentment and the peace she most earnestly felt within her heart. It was in this place that Marie discovered the inner solace allowing her to release her heart to the throes of an all-consuming love.

Here at *Schloss Finckenstein,* she had rejoined herself with the missing half of her soul. She once again felt complete and untainted. There was no need for her to slink back clandestinely to her Warsaw home under the veil of darkness, chased by a rising morning sun. There were no false illusions of propriety to upkeep. Marie need not avert her gaze from other women to whom she would be introduced at societal functions. She no longer had to play out the charade of devotion to her aged Polish *Starosta* husband. All she had to do here was to follow her heart, enjoy the moments of solitude stolen away with her Napoleon between his never-ending meetings, and revel in the fact that everyone - soldiers, officers, and diplomats alike - all knew her simply to be "the Emperor's Polish wife."

"My Napoleon," she responded, "how you spoil me with so many presents. Are you not aware you have already given me the greatest gift of all, that of your affections?"

"But, my love," Napoleon replied, "I had to force those affections upon you, for you first denied my heart so adamantly."

"Ah, but that was before I knew how true its pounding was," Marie answered. "Before I knew just how sweet your words and your thoughts could be! How sincere, how fascinating a man you truly are. So very different than any other man I had ever met."

"Well, my lovely Marie," he replied, "fascinating is a most appropriate word, in this case. For not only you, but your countrymen will be fascinated by this order I have had Talleyrand prepare late last night. Here, I will allow you to have a peek at it, but you must honor my request not to share its contents with anyone else. We must not ruin your countrymen's surprise, *eh?"*

Napoleon rose spryly from the bed and retrieved paperwork from a diplomatic satchel. Marie took the document from his hands and read through it quickly. Her face smiled delightfully, but did not break out into the ebullient beaming that he expected. No sign emerged of the grand elation that he hoped for, but he knew why.

"So this is what you referenced in the other document, the one creating the Polish Horse Regiment, as the *Duchy of Warsaw.*"

She continued to smile demurely as she passed the document back to him. He reached out, taking it from her hands. He grasped her wrist gently and pointed with his other hand toward the map at end of the document.

"Ah, *mon petite chou,*" he said, addressing her with the French affectionate term, "I thought perhaps you might misconstrue the most important aspect of this document. As soon as I defeat Bennigsen's Russian army once and for all, I intend to award all the lands taken from your country by the Prussians during the Partitions to the Duchy of Warsaw! Look at the map."

Marie looked at her Emperor's eyes, and the excitement that seemed to brew in them. Marie looked up at him, "I see, my love, but. do not understand what is this *Duchy of Warsaw?*"

"It is my gift to you," he said, as he took both her arms in his hands, "and to your people. They wish to be a sovereign nation once more. This is the first step along that path. This Duchy will be a new state in Europe. You have convinced me to take this bold and decisive move. The charm of your heart has brought forth this so quickly from me. You shall forever be remembered by your countrymen for your role in bringing this state into being."

Marie's pleasant demeanor for the first time seemed to be troubled with confusion. It drove off the radiance of her face's complexion, and replaced it with a clutter of concern.

"But, my Emperor," she said, "my countrymen do not wish to establish a duchy around our capital. They need Poland to be re-established rightfully as the sovereign kingdom it once was."

Napoleon released her from his grasp and pulled away. These proud words she uttered seemed to be anticipated by him, though clearly he hoped she would not have taken refuge in them. She sensed a snide response forthcoming from within him, as if he might forget for the moment to precisely which Pole he replied.

"Ah, your kingdom!" Napoleon muttered, his disposition so quickly spoiled by her words. "A kingdom so weak its neighbors carved it up like a fatted calf? The final slice because of its May Third Constitution, which your country thought to be the envy of all Europe? How long from its introduction to the elimination of the kingdom from the map altogether? Just the blink of an eye!"

Marie could see that she had unwittingly walked into the trap that was already set in his mind, perhaps by Talleyrand. Her words were those the Emperor surely expected to hear from Prince Poniatowski and the elders of the Poles. She feared her words had loosened an avalanche in his disposition, as quickly triggered and unexpectedly befallen as the great banks of snow she had once witnessed tumble down in the Tatras Mountains near Zakopane.

"I am sorry, my love, for my initial reaction," she appeased him. "It is a fine start, and one that will encourage all Poles to fight on alongside you. The return of the lands the Prussians had stolen from us is the sacred seed to the reconstitution of Poland. I am quite sure that those lands pilfered by Austria and Russia will follow in time from your certain victories in the coming years."

"Ah, my Marie," Napoleon said, taking her in his arms once more, "if only your countrymen will come to see this for what you have already, so elegantly, called *'The Sacred Seed of the Reconstitution of Poland.'* You have the tongue of a diplomat. Perhaps I should rid myself of that rascal Talleyrand and instead make you my Minister of All Diplomacy? Might you enjoy that?"

"I would enjoy it only if it meant I would be by your side wherever you were to travel," she said, pressing her face into his chest. "For I fear most losing you in battle, or having to watch as you ride out of Poland to return to Paris and Empress Josephine."

"Your French is wonderful," he changed the subject, "with such a delicate accent. It would disarm all the ministers of Europe, who would compete to steal you away. *Non, c'est impossible!* I will not tolerate that! So, I am stuck with the rascal Talleyrand!"

From our field quarters in Finckenstein

on the 6th day of April 1807.

We, Napoleon I, Emperor of the French

and King of Italy, have determined as follows:

Article 1. A Polish Light Cavalry (Chevaux-légers) Regiment of the Guard will be formed.

Article 2. Regiment will consist of four squadrons, each of two companies.

Article 3. Each company will consist of one captain, two lieutenants, two sub-lieutenants, one sergeant major, six sergeants, one corporal-quartermaster, ten corporals, ninety-six cavalrymen, three trumpeters, two blacksmiths.

Article 4. Regimental Staff will consist of one colonel, two French majors of the Guard, four squadron commanders, one quartermaster-treasurer, one French instructor-captain from the Guard, two French adjutant-majors from the Guard, four sub-adjutant-majors from among the Poles, who formerly were on duty in Legions in France, one standard-bearer, four surgeons, two of them 1st class and two 2nd or 3rd, one sub-instructor in the rank of sergeant major, one staff trumpeter, two trumpeter-corporals, one tailor, one breecher, one shoemaker, one gunsmith, one saddlemaker, one armourer, and two blacksmiths.

Article 5. To be enlisted into the Chevaux-leger Corps one has to be a landowner or the son of a landowner, be more than 18 years old, and less than 40, and come with his own horse, uniform, caparison and other equipment according to the regulations; men, who can not afford immediately deliver a horse, uniform, caparison and equipment, will be paid in advance. Horse has to be a maximum 4 feet and 9 inches, and a minimum 4 feet and 6 inches tall.

Article 6. Polish Chevaux-legers of the Guard will have to fulfill the same duties as Chasseurs of the Guard. They will be able to obtain food, forage, and payments, which will be established by the Colonel General, commanding officer of all cavalry of the Guard.

Article 7. Cost of the initial equipment, as will be established by the Administrative Board for those who have not enough money, 15 sous will be deducted daily until the termination of the pay.

Article 8. Administrative Board book-keeping and Registre-Matricule will be organized in the same fashion as in other cavalry regiments of the Guard.

Article 9. Men, who want to be enrolled in the Chevaux-legers of the Guard, have to immediately present themselves to Prince Poniatowski, director of the Department of War of the Duchy of Warsaw, and explain before him their serviceableness, according to the Article 5th. Next they have to present themselves to a Major chosen to organize the regiment, who – after examination – will incorporate candidates to the regiment, and note their age, description, country of origin, names of father and mother. Annotations will be presented for our acceptation.

Article 10. Our Ministry of War has obtained an order to fulfill this decree.

Part Three:

The Triumph of
The Peace at Tilsit
and Its Threat
at Wieliczka

You must not fight too often with one enemy, or you
will teach him all your art of war."

Napoleon Bonaparte

Chapter 14: Echoes of Eylau, March – June 1807

Napoleon, having had his army so severely depleted by the snow and ice-laden stalemate at Eylau, went about replenishing his manpower, with the sole intention of overpowering Bennigsen's forces once and for all. The Emperor pulled forward his soldiers already stationed in the western German states, and backfilled them with raw recruits taken directly from the military academies of Paris. Add to this thousands of Polish foot soldiers being trained for the infantry, in addition to the riders preparing for the Light Horse Regiment, and soon, the number of the Empire's forces was at 220,000 soldiers against Russian forces of only roughly 115,000 strong, including some 8,000 Cossacks. Even with the addition of 20,000 Prussians left available in fighting condition,[14] it was just a matter of time before Napoleon would finally engage and subdue the Tsar's army.

Despite the limited size of the lands of East Prussia, half of which the French by then already commanded, the Russians proved hard to pin down. Bonaparte's great fear was that Alexander, if threatened, would pull his forces back across the Niemen River and into the lands of Mother Russia. In that case, he had no intention of pursuing them. Still, something told Bonaparte that the Tsar would not dishonorably walk away from his conflict with the French, or for that matter, from his allegiance with the Prussian King Friedrich Wilhelm and his lovely Queen Louise. Napoleon knew the Tsar hungered for military glory above all else.

---

14 The Campaigns of Napoleon, Volume II, David Chandler, 1966, p. 189

Only two significant fortresses were left under the control of these Prussian monarchs: the Baltic port city of Danzig and the capital of East Prussia at Königsberg. Napoleon focused first on the taking of Danzig. Being situated at the mouth of the Vistula, it represented both a crucial port for resupply by the Russian ships coming out of St. Petersburg. Also, the city posed a threat as a staging site for his enemies to encircle behind and cut off the French forces in Poland and East Prussia. The French Emperor had planned to besiege the stronghold before Bennigsen's winter attack, but the Russians' bold stroke forced Napoleon to pull Marshal Lefebvre's forces south to reinforce Thorn. Bonaparte was forced to abandon his plans to surround Danzig until after the debacle at Eylau. Ten days after that battle was stalemated, Napoleon sent Marshal Lefebvre a note instructing him:

*"**Your glory is linked to the taking of Danzig:
you must go there.**"*[15]

Finally, the siege of Danzig began on 19 March 1807, when Marshal Lefebvre's 27,000 troops encamped outside the Baltic city's walls. The besieged port had only 60,000 inhabitants augmented by 14,400 Prussian troops under Count Friedrich Adolf von Kalckreuth, the Prussian general who had led his troops in defeat at the Battle of Auerstädt six months earlier.

French forces, including two divisions of Poles under General Jan Dąbrowski, encircled Danzig on the 20th of March. Three days later, the French guns opened fire on the city's walls. The following week, the ground thawed, and the digging of trenches up to the city's ramparts began.

The Russians refused to remain idle as the French besieged the critical port, which served as the gateway to the Vistula. They mustered 7,000 troops and sailed them from their port of Saint Petersburg across the Baltic, landing on the shores east of Danzig, intending to save the city from being besieged.

---

[15] Napoleonic Correspondence, 18 February 1807, *Foundation Napoléon Archives*

The Russian forces did not arrive until early May due to delays in arranging transportation for these troops with their allies from Britain and Sweden. By then, Lefebvre had already reinforced his own troops to defend against the threat of the Russians' relief plans for the city's garrison. While some fighting took place east of Danzig, the Tsar's relief forces were quickly defeated and withdrew without providing any significant aid.

With the Russian relief threat removed, the siege continued, eventually reaching its seventy-eighth day. Running low on provisions and facing an all-out onslaught by the besieging French forces, the Prussian Count von Kalckreuth realized his fate was sealed and negotiated for peace. On the 24th of May, his forces were allowed to march out of the city with full military honors. Two days later, Napoleon, *en route* to Danzig, scribbled off a note to his beloved mistress, Marie Walewska, whom he had left behind at *Schloss Finckenstein*:

"My sweet friend, the place of Danzig has capitulated, I know you will be happy to hear it from me. I'm leaving for Danzig, but I haven't forgotten my promise. Be calm and happy, because the horizon is brightening, and we will see each other again soon. This is my dearest wish."[16]

Napoleon personally entered the city on the first of June. For his marshal's superior efforts, he would later award Lefebvre the title of *"Duke of Danzig."*

June of 1807 continued with Napoleon's departure from Danzig to pursue the Russians in the field. He then sought to achieve his last remaining objective, that being the fall of the capital of Königsberg, where Friedrich Wilhelm and Queen Louise still took refuge. His greatest wish was to humiliate the monarchs

---

[16] Napoleonic Correspondence, 26 May 1807, *Foundation Napoléon Archives*

Bennigsen likewise knew, given the overall aggregation of forces under Napoleon, that his Russian army was significantly outnumbered. He looked for any opportunity to bring the levels of opposing forces closer to parity. Bennigsen sought to isolate and destroy Napoleon's individual marshals and their corps in battle by forcing them to engage the entire Russian army. The Russian Commander believed he had found his first opportunity to employ this strategy when Marshal Ney's Sixth Corps' forces were spotted outside the small river town of Guttstadt. Taking on a single corps of the French would prove to be a decisive tactic in theory, but disastrous in practice.

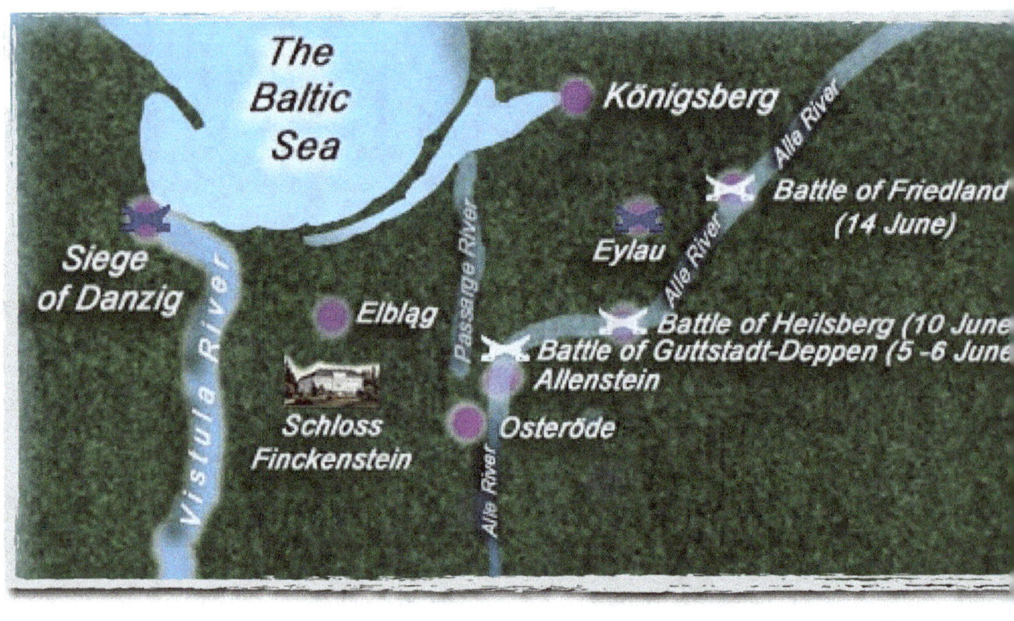

Figure 19: Battles along the Alle River after June 1, 1807

Chapter 15: Battles Along The Alle River

June, 1807

Napoleon entered Danzig on 1 June 1807. Afterward, he prepared to bring his newly reconstituted forces into direct conflict with Tsar Alexander's army. Napoleon's army swelled to 220,000 men in East Prussia, but he found himself in need of experienced leadership assistance, so he brought up Marshal André Masséna, the Duke of Rivoli. Masséna, a decade earlier in Italy, had served Bonaparte so brilliantly in battles against the Austrians that he became known as *l'Enfant chéri de la Victoire (the Dear Child of Victory)*. Marshal Masséna was given 30,000 troops to defend the *Grande Armée's* right wing, the area surrounding Warsaw. This freed Napoleon with the remaining 190,000 troops to pursue Bennigsen throughout East Prussia. There, the Emperor would be pitted against a combined remaining force of only 135,000 Russian and Prussian soldiers.

However, before Napoleon could position his forces to engage, the Russian commander Bennigsen struck first. By 2 June, Bennigsen had concentrated his troops in the town of Heilsberg, and from there he planned to strike at exposed units of the French Empire's army. On 5 June, the Russian commander located one of Napoleon's corps alone in the town of Guttstadt. Bennigsen planned to isolate and obliterate them with six columns of troops. The target was the famed Sixth Corps under Marshal Michel Ney.

It had been Ney who, with Marek Zaczek's assistance, had stumbled upon Bennigsen's audacious winter surprise movement only months earlier. In January, Marshal Ney led his Sixth Corps' soldiers in skirmishing against an overpowering force of 63,000 troops of the Russian army to slow their advance. This time, in early June, the Russians would attack his 17,000 men at Guttstadt, twelve miles southwest of the enemy camp at Heilsberg.

Guttstadt was a small town along the banks of the Alle River. Bennigsen first sent two small diversionary attacks against other French forces on the nearby Passarge River, running just west of the Alle. He sent Russian troops to engage Marshal Soult at Lomitten, and Prussians forces against Marshal Bernadotte at the town of Spanden. These attacks were mere engagements designed only to prevent those forces from moving east to aid the primary target, Marshal Ney.

The main Russian movement then crossed the Alle River at Guttstadt on the fifth of June, intending to surround Ney's outnumbered corps. However, the multiple Russian columns sent were poorly coordinated, allowing Ney to miraculously fight his way westward overland to the Passarge River. In typical fashion, Bennigsen greatly overstated his success to the Tsar:

"General Ney's corps is defeated, and General Roget, several officers, with about 2,000 rank and file, have been taken prisoners; the enemy's loss in killed amounts to 2,000; on our side is not very considerable." [17]

By the morning of the sixth, Ney's Sixth Corps was able to fight through the enemy and cross the Passarge at the town of Deppen over a single wooden bridge. They met up there with French forces sent forward from Osteröde, including the Imperial Polish Guard under the command of the newly promoted Lieutenant Colonel Marek Zaczek.

---

[17] "Napoleon's Polish Gamble, Christopher Summerville, 2005, page 116.

"Ah, Zaczek," Ney stated upon seeing him waiting on the west bank of the Passarge, "I have never been happier to see you and your Polish horsemen. Well, perhaps at Jena, that is true. But at least I finally get to address you as Lieutenant Colonel Zaczek."

"It appears, *mon Maréchal,*" Marek answered, "that you have an uncanny knack for finding the whole of the Russian army."

"Well, I will have to learn," Ney answered with a sly smile, "not to only utilize that talent when my Sixth Corps is all alone against the enemy's full army in the field. I suppose I should set this bridge alight before we have their company, *eh?*"

"Perhaps," Marek offered, "we should allow them to pass over and then set it ablaze. They would be trapped with their backs to the river, and we could have a turkey shoot."

"Ah, Zaczek," Ney said, "I don't think even the incompetent Russians would be foolish enough to make such a move. Perhaps that is a ploy we can try at another time, for today, there will be far too many of them to use that strategy."

Then Ney gave the order to set fire to the bridge. As this was done, its frame twisted and writhed like a tormented beast as the flames consumed its weathered wood. Soon, sections of red-hot planks broke free and fell, sizzling as they surrendered to the cold, slowly moving waters of the Passarge River below.

Bennigsen was outraged at his generals for not having destroyed Ney's Sixth Corps and allowing their escape with only minimal losses. One significant casualty of the diversionary attack at Spanden on the Passarge River was Marshal Bernadotte. He defeated the Prussian attack there, but in doing so, was struck high in the neck by a musket ball. His near-fatal wound removed him from service for the rest of Napoleon's Polish Campaign.

Napoleon was unsure of the enemy's next move. He wrote to another of his leaders, *the Iron Marshal*, Davout:

"What will the enemy do? Will he continue on to Allenstein while we still hold Deppen and Liebstadt?

If so, very unusual events may well take place…

No doubt you will select advantageous positions at Osteröde, from which you will be able to hold up the enemy should he advance thither. You are my extreme right wing. Until the enemy attacks you there my intention is to pivot on you. I am relying on your courage and staunchness - and even more on your guns and strong positions - to win us as much time as possible."[18]

---

[18] Correspondence, Volume XV, No. 12741 as sourced in The Campaigns of Napoleon, Volume II, David Chandler, 1966, page 190.

But Napoleon's concerns of an attack on Allenstein or at Osteröde did not materialize. Perhaps this was due to his own ingenuity, as he decided to take advantage of the Russians' ploy of using Cossacks to intercept messages from his command. Bonaparte directed that two riders carry false orders to Marshal Ney, relaying a fictional message from Napoleon's headquarters. He directed that they be sent along specific routes where, unknown to the couriers, they were likely to be intercepted by Cossack patrols. One rider stubbornly made it through to deliver his orders, defeating the deception. The second courier, however, was captured, and his message was surrendered as desired to the Russian high command.[19]

On 7 June, General Bennigsen read that fictional order stating that Marshal Davout was about to encircle Guttstadt and attack with 40,000 troops. Bennigsen immediately recalled all remaining Russian forces to Heilsberg, while sending all Prussian forces to Königsberg. He was reacting to a phantom movement, as Davout remained at Osteröde. The order was nothing more than a *ruse de guerre* conjured up by Napoleon, but with great effect.[20]

As the Emperor waited to see if Bennigsen had taken the bait, he wrote to the injured Marshal Bernadotte, directing him to get to safety:

"I learned with the greatest sadness that you had been injured. I hope that you do not waste a moment in going to Danzig or Marienburg. It is possible that I will make a move, and you know all the dangers attached to the rear of an army….

I hope for your speedy recovery and to see you again at the head of my army corps for the good of my service, but also for the particular interest that I take in everything that concerns you…

---

[19] The Campaigns of Napoleon, Volume II, David Chandler, 1966, page 190.

[20] "Napoleon's Polish Gamble, Christopher Summerville, 2005, page 117.

I am still guessing what the enemy wanted to do; This all seems like a fluke to me. Today I am gathering my infantry and cavalry reserves at Mohrungen, and I will try to find the enemy and engage them in a general battle, in order to put an end to them."[21]

By the next day, it was clear that the Russians had abandoned their offensive and were rapidly falling back to their fortifications a dozen miles down the Alle River at Heilsberg. Napoleon decided to take the fight to Bennigsen there. He believed that by driving the Russians from Heilsberg, he could cut them off from retreating north to the Prussian capital, Königsberg.

On the morning of 10 June, Napoleon sent an advance team of cavalry to Heilsberg under his flamboyant brother-in-law, Marshal Joachim Murat. His orders were to locate enemy redoubts or other strongholds and to skirmish lightly with the enemy to hold them there until the bulk of *La Grande Armée* could arrive. Murat instead began a series of frontal assaults, charging directly at the Russian strongholds there. His charges were repeatedly repelled, and he soon began to rebuke the leadership under him for their failure to overtake the Russians, but never accepted that his own decision to launch the direct assaults was ill-advised.

However, the marshal was no coward. He led these cavalry charges of Hussars and Chasseurs himself, making a splendid target in his vain all-white dress uniform set off by red Moroccan leather boots. He could not be any more unmistakable on the battlefield if he wore a bullseye on his chest. He became engaged in horse-to-horse melees with a superior number of Russian Dragoons and had to fight for his life. Murat had two mounts shot out from under him, with a red Moroccan leather boot left in a stirrup of the second dead horse.[22]

---

[21] Napoleonic Correspondence, 7 June 1807, *Foundation Napoléon Archives*

[22] "Napoleon's Polish Gamble, Christopher Summerville, 2005, page 122.

Later in the day, as Napoleon arrived at Heilsberg, he quickly assessed that the Russian positions were too well entrenched to be taken by direct assault, even with arriving infantry supporting Murat's cavalry. Instead, he engaged the enemy only to occupy them as he began flanking to encircle the city.

Bennigsen was quick to recognize this threat and planned yet another evacuation. At dawn on 11 June, both sides suspended the engagement to tend to their battlefield casualties. Both dead and wounded alike had been stripped clean in the overnight darkness by the locals of anything remotely valuable or able to be sold. The toll of dueling armies marching through the countryside had proven dire indeed for both villagers and peasants alike.

Throughout the eleventh of June, there was light fighting and a continuation of Napoleon's flanking maneuvers, but as soon as darkness fell, the Russians exited the town to move even further down river. The Tsar's army lived to fight another day. The French entered Heilsberg the next morning before dawn to find it empty of enemy combatants, but still well provisioned. Napoleon, having won Heilsberg, then planned to surround Königsberg some twenty or so miles to the north. He knew not where Bennigsen had fled, but was intent on cutting the commander off from that capital.

That same afternoon, Napoleon wrote to Marie Walewska:

"My sweet friend, everything is going as I planned, we are on the heels of the enemy, and the Polish division is filled with enthusiasm and courage. The day is approaching for a reunion that I call for with all my heart, where we can live for each other."[23]

Napoleon's reference to *"the Polish division"* was their agreed-upon code that Marie was free to inform her governess, Magdalena, that her son, Lieutenant Colonel Marek Zaczek, remained safe and uninjured.

---

[23] Napoleonic Correspondence, 12 June 1807, *Foundation Napoléon Archives*

Chapter 16: The Decisive Battle of Friedland

June 14, 1807

Bennigsen, having abandoned Heilsberg, led his troops along the eastern bank of the meandering Alle to the town of Friedland, some thirty-two miles downriver. Once there, he could cross his army over the single wooden bridge to enter the town on the river's western bank. From there, he could choose to take the road to Königsberg or take another route to return to the safety of Russian soil by crossing the Niemen River. After his most recent losses, he commanded only sixty thousand men, including the Cossacks under the Russian General Platov's command.

The Russian commander's only hope was to use his full army to isolate and destroy an individual Napoleonic Marshal's corps, as he had attempted to do against Marshal Ney at Guttstadt a week earlier. Even given his failure there, Bennigsen did not hesitate to employ that same tactic again when his scouts spotted Marshal Lannes' Reserve Guard of only 16,000 men across the river on the afternoon of 13 June. Bennigsen immediately began to move his troops across the town's single wooden bridge, but the narrowness of it and the streets of Friedland made for a slow crossing. By late that evening, only 10,000 of his troops had moved to the western bank. Bennigsen then ordered three pontoon bridges to be built overnight by his sappers (engineers) so that his soldiers could more rapidly engage the French at dawn on the 14th.

Marshal Lannes had a clear view of the size of the enemy forces on the opposite bank of the Alle. He knew time was not on his side and needed assistance as soon as possible. Lannes sent a message off to the Emperor, telling the courier:

"Ride your horse into the ground if you have to, but tell the Emperor we are fighting the entire Russian army." [24]

Lannes knew two things to be true: first, his job was to fight delaying tactics to lure as many Russian troops as possible across the river and through the town of Friedland. The second was as old as warfare itself; never fight with your back to a river.

Marshal Lannes proved to be masterful in employing his delaying tactics against the ever-increasing number of Russians on his side of the Alle. French reserves began to arrive overnight. The Russian cannons opened fire at three o'clock that morning. Marshal Ney's Sixth Corps, eager to re-engage the Russians after the battle of Guttstadt-Deppen, arrived shortly afterward. When Napoleon arrived at midday, he scoured the western banks before him, and seeing the bulk of the Russian army there, said:

"We won't catch the enemy making a mistake like this twice." [25]

Bennigsen had badly mistaken how fast the French Corps could move. The French had amassed 80,000 troops west of the town. Napoleon noticed that of the 50,000 Russians by then on the western bank, they not only had the river itself to their back, but they were bisected by the steep banks of the Millstream - a rivulet running across the battlefield. The Russians made one final error. The three pontoon bridges constructed overnight were all placed not far from the town bridge. This would force any retreating Russian forces to funnel through the town's close-quartered streets to gain access to their crossings.

---

[24] *"Napoleonic Wars: The Battle of Friedland 1807,"* Epic History TV

[25] *"Napoleonic Wars: The Battle of Friedland 1807,"* Epic History TV

With his staff having requested to delay the onset of hostilities until the next morning, Napoleon replied:

"Today is a happy day - it is the seventh anniversary of the Battle of Marengo. I am going to beat the Russians today just as I beat the Austrians then!"[26]

The Emperor ordered the attack to commence at 5:30 pm that evening of the 14th of June. This caught Bennigsen off guard, who assumed it to be too late in the day to begin an engagement.

Napoleon's decision proved to be extremely consequential as Bennigsen, once more having failed to obliterate a stray corps of the French *Grande Armée*, realized he faced the full strength of his enemy's forces. He ordered his troops to begin retreating back across to the eastern bank of the Alle River.

French guns sounded in three successive salvos at 5:30 that evening as the signal for Marshal Ney's forces to emerge from the cover of the Sortlach Woods. An astounded Bennigsen was forced to countermand his "retreat" order to "engage the enemy in battle."

Ney's Sixth Corps was awarded the pressing of the initial assault - a bit of revenge for Bennigsen having twice attempted to crush them. The Emperor's direction was clear:

"This is the objective: advance, looking neither right nor left, bore into this thick mass of Russians, cost what it may."[27]

The French forces formed a massive arch of a front spanning from the village of Sortlach in the south, up to the village of Posthenen near its center, and then on to the village of Heinrichsdorf in the north. The Russians fought fiercely, supported by cannon fire from their guns positioned across the river. Ney's Corps was initially driven back, but aided by their comrades, it soon recovered the offensive.

---

[26] The Campaigns of Napoleon, Volume II, David Chandler, 1966, pages 202 - 203.

[27] *"Napoleonic Wars: The Battle of Friedland 1807,"* Epic History TV

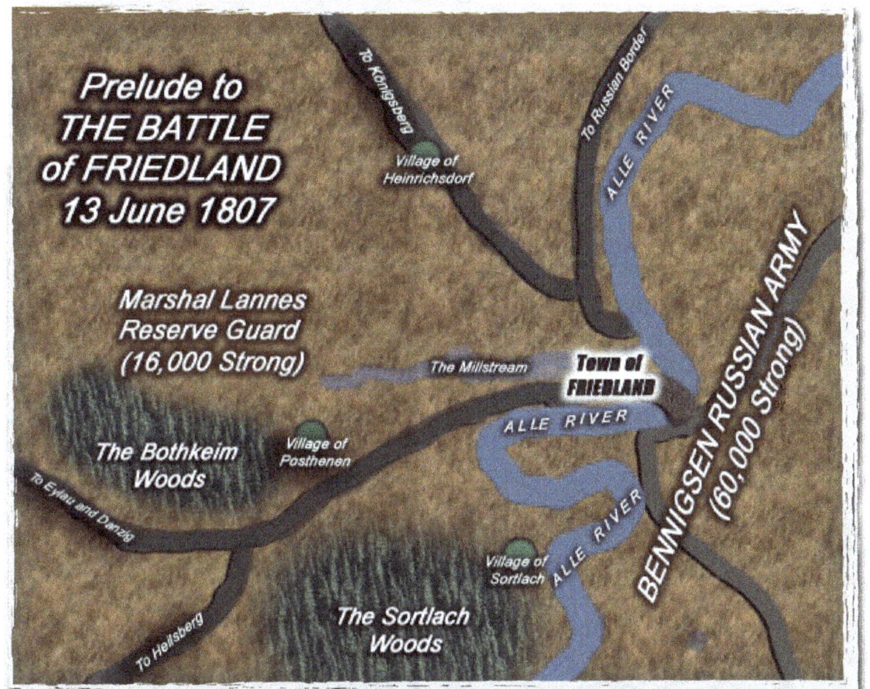

**Figure 21: The Mismatch of Forces before
The Battle of Friedland**

In the north, near the village of Heinrichsdorf, began massive engagements of cavalry on both sides, pitting the French Hussars against units of Russian Dragoons. Over the next several hours, the French cavalry and infantry would squeeze the Russians up against the river, all the while under a withering French artillery bombardment that decimated the town of Friedland and the lines of Russian soldiers alike. French canister shot was brought to bear on Russian infantry, forcing many no alternative but to flee into the waters of the Alle River to escape. Many Russians drowned there, weighed down by their weapons and water-soaked uniforms.

After only three hours of fighting, the town and all four bridges crossing the Alle River were ablaze. The Russian forces were cut off and trapped against the river. By the time the battle ceased, a third of the entire Russian army had been decimated. The Emperor finally had his decisive victory over Tsar Alexander.

During the battle, Marek Zaczek was commanding one of the units of the Polish Light Horse Brigade near the village of Heinrichsdorf, north of the Millstream. They were assigned to patrol areas near the river, thought to have been cleared of the enemy. They entered an area by a small copse of trees when they were suddenly attacked by a band of half a dozen Cossacks. Before they even fully realized the enemy horsemen were upon them, two of their companions were cut down by savage sabre strokes.

Marek led his force to engage the Cossacks and drive them away from the French forces encamped nearby. Mieczysław Wieczorek, the master swordsman, engaged one of the horsemen, slashing open the Cossack's chest. After which, their remaining number, having lost the element of surprise, retreated to a deep but dangerously negotiable ford they had used to cross the waters of the River Alle.

"What do we do, Lieutenant Colonel?" asked Antoni Pilarczyk, as they pulled up on the river's bank. The Cossacks were deep in the Alle's waters on horseback. A pair slid off their horses and grasped the animals' tails as they swam. Just then, Antoni's younger brother Edziu, full of rage, blindly followed the Cossacks into the waters of the Alle through the deep ford.

"Well, Antoni," Marek answered, "it appears your brother has decided your question for us. We will pursue, of course!"

Then Marek, Antoni, and Mieczysław led their mounts from the shore to the eastern bank of the Alle. Only Klęczeć Sałeh stayed behind and returned to Heinrichsdorf.

Four on five, Marek thought as he watched the Cossacks emerge from the river ahead of them and immediately make for the dense forest not far beyond. They were well away from the rest of the Russian army forces, so the four Poles climbed out of the river and pursued the five Cossacks into the thick of the woods. As they did, they found themselves set on by the Cossacks in ambush. All men already had their sabres drawn, but within the confined space of the dense forest, the swing of their blades was greatly restricted.

Mieczysław seemed to be dealing with the constraint of the forest best, as he changed the slashing stroke of his blade for a more compact stabbing motion. His sabre soon impaled another Cossack's chest, driving him from his saddle. This evened up the fight to four on four. Edziu copied Mieczysław's style and soon ran another through the stomach.

Marek fought with an enemy, blade on blade, but in the throes of that life and death struggle never got a good look at the Cossack's face. Neither man gained any advantage over the other, and despite the vigor of both men, no serious wounds were landed. Soon, their horses parted from each other to avoid crashing into the trees. It was only then, as his opponent separated from him, that Marek clearly saw his face. He was amazed to see it was none other than the Cossack Bohun, his wife Maya's cousin.

As Marek looked on in surprise at Bohun, Antoni dropped a third Cossack. It was then four of them against only the two remaining Cossacks. Marek saw Bohun realize they were in grave danger, as the Cossack alerted his companion.

"Fadeyka," Bohun called out, followed by some words in Ukrainian that Marek assumed meant *let's get the hell out of here.*

Edziu began to give chase to the pair, and closed in from behind on Bohun, clearly having the angle to cut off and slay the retreating Cossack, but Marek instead called him off.

"They have had enough," Marek shouted, "and want us only to follow them back, perhaps into a trap. Let these two go, we need to get back to our unit before the dark of night fully falls."

As Marek said this, he could see Bohun turn his mount to stare him down with a snarled expression upon his face. Marek remembered that the Cossack spoke near-perfect Polish from their brief encounter at Christmas in Warsaw. He surely heard Marek's words. Bohun's sneer seemed to clearly say, *I don't need your charity, Marek Zaczek, killer of Cossacks. Don't expect me to return the favor when we meet again and the tables are turned.*

The two Cossacks rode off through the forest at an unimaginable rate of speed. Their three companions lay on the deeply bloodied pine straw forest floor, slowly dying from their wounds. Another had died in the initial attack across the river.

As Marek led the others back through the raging waters across the ford in the Alle, he looked up to see thick smoke rising above the town of Friedland. Its buildings and bridges were all ablaze. A lifeless Russian corpse floated past him. Drowned infantry, he could see from the uniform insignia. Poor bastard, just another Russian soldier who would die from the onset of gross panic during a battle that did not go their way. The Russians appeared to have been told great lies about the French treatment of prisoners. So many of them would rather fight to the death or even take the high chance of drowning in the Alle rather than surrender.

"Edziu," Marek called out to his companion, "why on earth did you follow those Cossacks so rashly across that deep ford? You could have been killed had we not followed!"

"Because they slaughtered Jan Kalinski back there in their surprise attack," he answered, as if that explained everything.

"But this is war, you know that. Was Kalinski so close a friend of yours," Marek asked, "that you would risk your own life in revenging his?"

"No," Edziu demurred, "but Jan owed me a lot of money from gambling at Baccarat. A small fortune, in fact. I will never collect a *złoty* of it now. Someone had to die over that gross outrage, it could not be allowed to stand."

"Well," Marek replied, "that explains everything, of course. Why not gamble with all our lives as well as your own?"

As they returned to the western shore, Marek heard Bohun's voice in his mind taunting him:

Marek Zaczek, Cossack killer. You are the only one of your party who did not kill a Cossack this day. I will make you regret allowing me to live. It will prove to be your great mistake. The day will come when you least expect and then you'll pay with your life.

After the victory at Friedland, Napoleon sent several notes to the Empress Josephine in Paris. First, he wrote:

"Everything is fine here. The Battle of Friedland decided everything. The enemy is confused, defeated, extremely weakened. My health is good and my army is superb. Farewell, mon amie. Be cheerful and happy."[28]

---

[28] Napoleonic Correspondence, 13 July 1807, *Foundation Napoléon Archives*

Figure 23: Battle of Friedland Force Map (14 June 1807)

Napoleon later followed with:

"My children have worthily celebrated the anniversary of Marengo. The Battle of Friedland will be just as famous and glorious for my people… It is the worthy sister of Marengo, Austerlitz and Jena."[29]

It is clear from these communications that the Emperor was jubilant in his victory over Alexander, but even so, he worried about his depressed wife's state of mind. He reassured her of his health and, in the final note of this sequence, reasserted his disdain for his soon-to-be only remaining enemy. That foe, who would prove to pose the most dangerous threat, was the British.

---

[29] Correspondence 12758 sourced to The Campaigns of Napoleon, Volume II, David Chandler, 1966, page 206.

After the Battle of Friedland was won, Bennigsen had no hope of making his way to Königsberg. In fact, that capital would fall two days later, on the 16th of June to Marshal Soult. On that occasion, Napoleon would again write to his Empress:

"Mon amie,
I sent you… yesterday… news of the battle of Friedland.
Since then, I have continued to pursue the enemy.
Königsberg, which is a city of eighty thousand souls,
is in my power. I found there many buildings, many stores, and
finally more than one hundred and sixty thousand rifles
coming from England.
Farewell, mon amie. My health is perfect, although a little cold
from the sun and the [serene] bivouac. Be happy and cheerful.
All to you"[30]

Napoleon knew he had finally struck the *coup de grâce* against the Tsar's forces in that battle at Friedland. There was no viable way for Alexander to continue his support of King Friedrich Wilhelm and Queen Louise of Prussia. All that was left was for the young Russian leader's capitulation request to arrive. That came to pass on the 19th, when the Tsar's envoy, Prince Lobanoff, rode into Napoleon's headquarters to request an armistice. It was agreed to, and a four-week ceasefire began on the twenty-third.[31] All that remained for the French Emperor was to negotiate a long-lasting peace that would unite all of Continental Europe against his last remaining enemy - the British.

---

[30] Napoleonic Correspondence, 16 June 1807, *Foundation Napoléon Archives*

[31] The Campaigns of Napoleon, Volume II, David Chandler, 1966, pages 206.

In the days after the battle, Bennigsen attempted to rally his troops to the north and east of Friedland, but was continually harassed by pursuing French cavalry under Marshal Murat. Instead, he returned with 40,000 troops, all that was then left of his army, to the northeast, where he would lead them back into his homeland across the Niemen River, the traditional Polish-Russian border.

As Napoleon and Talleyrand jointly pondered and finalized the terms of their great peace accord, Murat, having trailed the Russians to the Niemen River, rested his riders on its banks at a small Prussian border town soon to be made famous over all of civilization. The world would soon learn the name of Tilsit.

Figure 24: Napoleon, Victor at Friedland (14 June 1807)

Chapter 17: Tilsit
The Pinnacle of Peace
June 25th - July 9th, 1807

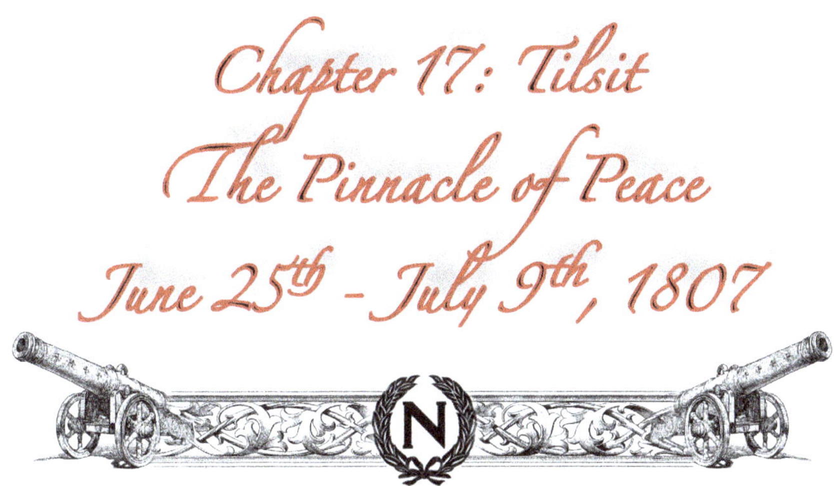

Napoleon had achieved all his goals save one - to strike up an amiable relationship with the youthful Tsar Alexander. He knew this could perhaps truly be his most difficult undertaking, having defeated the ruler's army so devastatingly. The French Emperor had no intentions of crossing the Niemen River to invade Russia itself, just the opposite. He desired to conquer the Russians' hearts and minds, not their lands. In this vein, he went out of his way to treat the conquered Tsar Alexander as an equal.

Tilsit sits on the banks of the Niemen River. It separated the East Prussian kingdom, and in fact, Poland, from the lands of Russia. The town was an old Teutonic Knight enclave, and Napoleon could have hosted Alexander in the castle known as *Schalauer Haus,* founded in 1288, certainly a worthy historic site. However, that would have required the Tsar to enter into those Prussian lands so recently conquered by the French. Instead of rubbing that defeat in the Tsar's nose, Napoleon decided to have a large raft floated in the middle of the Niemen in neutral waters. Upon it, he had built a handsome apartment with two doors, one facing conquered Prussia, the other the shores of the expanse of Russia. It was upon this float that Napoleon would engage Alexander as a total equal to conclude a peace that had minimal impact on Russia, but severely punished the Prussians.

It must be recalled that Napoleon had greatly looked forward to meeting Alexander after the Battle of Austerlitz in December of 1805, only to learn from the Austrian Emperor that the Tsar had withdrawn back to Russia. A year and a half later, on the 25th of June, 1807, the two Emperors finally met for the first time. Alexander's first words to Napoleon were reported as being,

"I hate the English as much as you do yourself."[32]

To which Napoleon answered,

"If that is the case, then peace is already made."[33]

The two Emperors embraced and then had a long conversation amidst the waters of the Niemen. They struck not only an amiable tone, but one more akin to that of long-lost, reunited friends, and agreed to meet over the next several days in the town of Tilsit itself. After the meeting, Napoleon wrote to Talleyrand,

"Monsieur Prince of Benevento,

I have just seen the Emperor of Russia, in the middle of the Niemen, on a raft where a beautiful flag had been raised. Tomorrow, the Emperor introduces me to the King of Prussia and is coming to stay in town. To this end, I neutralized the city of Tilsit. I very much hope that you come here quickly. I refrain from telling you more, thinking that it will not be long before you arrive here."[34]

By "neutralizing" Tilsit, Napoleon made it equally welcoming to the Tsar as to himself. Napoleon then anticipated humbling Friedrich Wilhelm III, King of Prussia, the man who had audaciously initiated this war, and forced the Emperor to chase his troops across East Prussia. Napoleon was eager for revenge.

---

[32] "Napoleon's Polish Gamble, Christopher Summerville, 2005, page 147.

[33] The Campaigns of Napoleon, Volume II, David Chandler, 1966, pages 206.

[34] Napoleonic Correspondence, 25 June 1807, *Foundation Napoléon Archives*

Napoleon and Alexander met over the next two weeks until the Peace of Tilsit was signed on the 7th of July. Each day was spent reviewing the very same French and Russian troops who had been attempting to destroy each other for months. At one point, Napoleon pinned a *Légion d'honneur* medal, taken from his own uniform, on a Russian soldier.

Perhaps the most interesting turn of events was when Friedrich Wilhelm III, after enduring the cold, harsh welcome of Napoleon, unleashed his secret weapon, his wife, Queen Louise of Mecklenburg-Strelitz. Napoleon's letters to his Empress seem to reflect a growing regard for the Prussian queen.

"I have received your letter of June 25. I saw with sorrow that you were selfish, and that the successes of my arms would be unattractive to you, if the little Baron de Kepen did not hope of a few little visits. This is ugly! I'm doing well.

It is interesting to note that *"Baron de Kepen"* was one of his unusual nicknames for Josephine's private parts. He continued,

The beautiful Queen of Prussia is to come and dine with me today. I am well and very much wish to see you again, when fate allows it. However, it is possible that it will not be long before it happens. Farewell, mon amie, a thousand pleasant things."[35]

Napoleon later wrote to Josephine:

"Mon amie, the Queen of Prussia, dined at my house yesterday. I had to defend myself from the fact that she wanted to force me to make a few more concessions to her husband: but I was gallant and stuck to my policy. She is very kind. To give you the details would be impossible for me without taking too long. When you read this letter, peace with Prussia and Russia will be concluded and Jerome recognized as king of Westphalia with three million population. All this I do for you alone.

---

[35] Napoleonic Correspondence, 6 July 1807, *Foundation Napoléon Archives*

Farewell, mon amie; I love you and
want to know you are content and happy. "[36]

It is clear Napoleon had not given into the charms of Queen Louise. While she used her wiles to plead for leniency in the awarding of Prussian lands to Poland during the final peace settlement, the Emperor refers in the last note that his brother, Jerome, will became the King of Westphalia. These, too, were lands taken from Prussia in the western half of their country.

---

[36] Napoleonic Correspondence, 7 July 1807, *Foundation Napoléon Archives*

In addition to the lands of Westphalia being stripped from Prussia, all Polish lands held by Prussia are to be combined to form the Grand Duchy of Warsaw. In total, the Kingdom of Prussia was reduced by one-half of its land holdings. It is clear Napoleon had never forgiven the Prussians for sharpening their swords against the stone steps of the French Embassy in Berlin in 1806.

As Marie Walewska predicted, the Poles' response was mixed. While great joy and pride were taken in the restored lands, resentment lingered that the state was not fully reconstituted as the country of Poland. Nor were the Poles satisfied with the Grand Duchy not being sovereign; instead, it fell under the rule of the king of its neighbor, Saxony. Despite all this, the Poles choked down their concerns and pledged to support Napoleon.

Marie Walewska continued to write Napoleon and profess her love for him even while he negotiated the peace at Tilsit. A few days afterward, Napoleon wrote to her saying,

> *Madam, I received your letter. I am touched by the feelings it contains. You know how many ways you are dear to me. Count on it and never doubt it. Be cheerful and happy.*[37]

Still, the day that Marie feared most drew near. Napoleon will soon be on his triumphant journey back to Paris and his Empress Josephine. He wrote to his wife,

> *"I arrived yesterday at 5 o'clock in the evening in Dresden, in very good health, although I stayed a hundred hours in the car, without going out. I am here with the King of Saxony, with whom I am very happy. So I am closer to you than half the way. It may be that one of these beautiful nights, I fall into Saint Cloud like a jealous person, I warn you. Farewell, mon amie. I will be very pleased to see you."*[38]

---

[37] Napoleonic Correspondence, 13 July 1807, *Foundation Napoléon Archives*

[38] Napoleonic Correspondence, 18 July 1807, *Foundation Napoléon Archives*

Marie Walewska awaited Napoleon to stop and spend one final night with her at *Schloss Finckenstein* on his way to Dresden, but he broke her heart by not doing so. Yet it seems the closer he drew to his home and his Empress, Napoleon cannot entirely rid himself of his feelings for his Polish mistress.

Is it because she has bored deep into his psyche? Is she more than just a feminine comfort, a distraction of companionship during the lonely undertaking of a distant war? Time would tell, but it was clear to Napoleon that she had developed a deep romantic bond to him. The Emperor wrote to Marie upon his return to Paris:

"My sweet and dear Marie,
you who love your country so much, you will understand with
what joy I find myself in France, after almost a year of absence.
This joy would be complete if you were here, but I have you in
my heart. The Assumption is your feast and my birthday: it is a
double reason for our souls to be in unison on that day. You
certainly wrote to me, as I do when sending you my wishes;
they are the first, let us hope that many others
will follow them, for many years to come.

Goodbye, my sweet friend, you will come and join me.
It will be soon, when business allows me the freedom to call you.

Believe in my unalterable affection."[39]

Napoleon will keep her close to his heart, just as she does him. Their relationship is far from over. In Poland, Marie is seen as the quintessential patriot, making the ultimate sacrifice for her country. Only she knows that the true sacrifice was not in the yielding to the Emperor of her entire body, *au contraire,* the most painful act was in surrendering to him her heart.

---

[39] Napoleonic Correspondence, 25 July 1807, *Foundation Napoléon Archives*

Chapter 18: Wieliczka
The Peril to The Peace
July, 1807

During the second week of July 1807, just after the peace was signed at Tilsit, Magdalena received in Warsaw a most disturbing correspondence from the field surgeon, third-class, Judasz Zdrajca. It explained that Magdalena's son, Lieutenant Colonel Marek Zaczek, has been attacked by brigands and severely wounded on a mission escorting Princess Izabela Czartoryska from her Palace at Pulawy to her country estate at Sieniawa. The note said he clung to life, and time was of the essence for her to attend her son there. Furthermore, the surgeon said he had taken the liberty of arranging a transport to carry her to her son's side. The coach would arrive within the hour.

When Magdalena broke down upon reading the note, her daughter-in-law came to comfort her.

"What is it, *Matka?*" Maya asked.

Magdalena allowed her to read the note. Maya gasped.

"I do not understand," Marek's wife said, confused by all that was happening so quickly. "Princess Izabela is our protectress. How is it she has not written us or sent a messenger of her own?"

"The note is very cryptic," Magdalena admitted, "it does not explain. Perhaps the Princess herself is gravely wounded. Or even dead. *Jezus Maryja i Józef,* I pray to you to protect them all."

"What will you do?" Maya asked.

"I must ready myself to depart," Magdalena answered. "I cannot allow my Marek to perish alone. You must come with me."

"How I want to," Maya said, tears forming in her eyes, "but I must stay here with the children. I am still nursing Bohun's child, Orest, or I would leave them all in Ewelina's care."

It was as if the mention of Ewelina drew her into the room. It was unusual that on this day, she had chosen to stay in the house.

"I will go with you, *Siostra,*" Ewelina said. "I was in the hall and heard everything. I can not allow you to travel alone. It is too dangerous, as Sieniawa is in the Austrian province of Galicia."

"Oh, Ewelina, *dziękuję bardzo,*" Magdalena said with great relief. "I thought to ask you, but, oh, you've been so distant since…" Magdalena did not finish the sentence, wanting not to reopen any old wounds.

"This is your time of need," Ewelina said, "and I must be there with you. I will go pack some things for us both."

With this, Ewelina moved away from them to the stairs. Maya looked very troubled.

"What is it, child?" Magdalena queried.

"This is all so rash," Maya said. "Perhaps you should contact the Countess. She can confirm this with General Duroc…"

"I had the same thought," Magdalena said, "but the Countess Marie is still at Kamieniec. Even if I went directly to General Duroc, who really does not know me very well, that could take hours. Hours Marek may not have. No, I must put my faith in the Lord. He will protect me."

Yet Maya remained skeptical. Something did not feel right.

"I am worried," she protested. "Ewelina seems to have had such a rapid change of heart."

"I prayed that she would for so long," Magdalena confessed. "Perhaps this is the Almighty answering my petitions. Who am I to second-guess her sincerity?

Maya dropped her head, as if in great shame. She felt embarrassed for not accepting Ewelina's sincerity as Christianly as her troubled mother-in-law had.

"I am sorry, *Matka,*" Maya said, "but it seems so strange to hear nothing from Marek for so long, and then to have this occur so suddenly. No, you are right, go to him, on behalf us both. Carry my love to him."

"Will you pray with me, while Ewelina packs our things?" Magdalena asked. "Perhaps a Rosary to the Blessed Virgin Mary for our safe travels, and of course, for Marek's life to be spared."

"Yes, of course," Maya answered, "I will get your beads."

Within the hour, the coach arrived, and Magdalena and Ewelina departed. A few hours later, they came to the border crossing into Galicia. After a brief delay, when the proper papers were presented along with the customary bribe, the coach was allowed entrance into the Austrian province. Once across, however, the driver waited, much to Magdalena's growing impatience.

"Driver," she called, "*Proszę,* my son is dying. We need to get to Sieniawa as quickly as we can."

"I am instructed to wait for your fellow rider," came the response. "Here, he approaches now."

A few seconds later, the coach door opened, and a man in a long gray overcoat and cape entered. He removed his top hat out of customary respect for the women.

"Doctor Olszewski," Magdalena said in shock, having not seen the man for many years. "How did you know my Marek was in dire need of your care?"

"Dzień dobry, Pani Magdalena," he said. Then, turning his head, he added, "Driver, take us to Wieliczka, post haste."

"No, we must go to Sieniawa," Magdalena objected, then a realization came over her, and tears flooded her eyes. "My Marek is no more! His corpse has already been taken to Wieliczka!"

Magdalena began to wail a pitiful stream of sorrow. Her hands covered her face but failed to hold back her tears, which slipped through her fingers like the opportunities of a wasted life.

"Pani Zaczek," Doctor Olszewski said soothingly as he produced a bottle from his interior pocket. "Here, drink this. Three swallows, *proszę*. It will help to calm you."

"No, no!" Magdalena protested.

Ewelina reached for the medicine and slowly administered it to her sister-in-law. After Magdalena managed her third swallow, Ewelina placed the bottle to her lips and took a heavy pull herself.

"Pani," the doctor continued, "your son is unharmed. I hate to tell you that you have been the victim of a ruse. Marek is out of touch from his unit, currently escorting your Countess Walewska from *Schloss Finckenstein* back to Warsaw. She stayed there hoping that the Emperor might spend one last night with her, but she was sadly disappointed when he passed her over in his haste to return to Paris and his wife, Empress Josephine." He grinned broadly, reveling the Countess' heartbreaking misery.

"Marek is safe. Thank the Lord," Magdalena was relieved. "Then why this subterfuge? Why do you take us to Wieliczka against our will?"

"It is not against my will at all, Magda," Ewelina said, calling her sister-in-law by the peasant name she once bore there. "In fact, it is I who helped the good doctor arrange all this."

"To what end?" asked Magdalena. "Why on earth would you allow me to fear my son might perish? Even if only for a few hours. Do you realize the pain I have endured in that time?"

"The pain you have endured?" Ewelina scoffed, her words salted with bitterness, "perhaps it was necessary to give you a taste of what I have had to endure three times over for many months now due to the actions of your son."

"*Pani* Zaczek," Doctor Olszewski said, "I want you to relax. Allow the laudanum to calm you. Count Von Arndt only wishes to have you return to the *folwark* for a brief stay."

"Count Von Arndt?" Magdalena repeated. "The man detests me. He is the reason I fled Kraków to Warsaw. You know this!"

"Indeed I do," the doctor admitted, "but the man is also my longtime employer. I am greatly indebted to him. Delivering you to him brings at least some of those arrears into settlement. But relax, the Count has assured me that no harm will come to you."

The coach rode all night, stopping only briefly at dawn to rest and water the team of horses. Throughout most of that time, Magdalena fell into a deep sleep given her intake of the laudanum, but the following day could not be induced to swallow even the smallest further dose of the medicine. While she was relieved that her son was uninjured, her mind could not rest at wondering what the Austrian Count had in store for her. It also irked her that Ewelina, who had lived so many years in Warsaw under her roof, could so readily agree to turn her over to this man.

As they came onto the grounds of the *folwark* they were escorted by a dozen horsemen.

"Who are these riders?" asked Magdalena.

"These are some of the Count's guards," professed the doctor. "They make up his security since you were last here. A man of his great wealth draws many who only wish to rob him of it."

The grounds remained mostly unchanged from what Magdalena remembered. The manor house where she had worked and had been forcibly taken against her will by Duke Sdanowicz appeared unchanged. But the Count was nowhere to be seen. Slightly up the hill stood the guest house that the Duke had built, hoping one day to have the honor of hosting the Austrian Emperor. That honor did not come to pass before the Count bilked him of it all - the mine, the grounds, the structures, and his title. That guest house was where Magdalena had once been imprisoned, as she guessed she would be once more.

The doctor led them from the coach up to the guest house, where they were taken upstairs to the very same suite in which Magda, as she was then known, had been held against her will.

"You will wait here," the doctor said to her, "until the Count can make time to come and see you. I know you will be more than comfortable, both of you."

The last few words drew protest from Ewelina. "I do not intend to stay here with her…" pointing her finger accusingly at her sister-in-law whom she had betrayed so brashly.

"You do not have any say in the matter," said the doctor. "The Count does not fully trust you as of yet, my dear. He can not afford to have you working counter to his plans in the meanwhile.

"What plans?" asked Magdalena.

"That is a question to ask the Count," Doctor Olszewski said avoiding her gaze. Then he locked them both in the chamber. Magdalena moved to the window to watch the doctor walk the path down to the manor house. It was then she noticed below the window a cart of hay had been pushed up against the ground floor wall. It seemed all too convenient.

All they had to do was break the window and drop down into the soft hay of the wagon. Magdalena thought it to have been placed there to entice them to try and do just that? Why would he desire to facilitate their attempt to escape in any way? She knew it was far better to trust her instincts than to trust the Count's intentions.

The two women then avoided each other, despite their close quarters, and waited until nightfall. When dusk began to fall, Count Maximilian Von Arndt came from the manor house to the guest quarters. The door was unlocked from the outside and he entered the room, while two of his guards blocked the doorway.

"Witaj w domu, Magdalena i Ewelina," he said, welcoming them home in Polish. "I have been waiting so long for this little reunion."

"This was never my home," Magdalena said, "just a prison then, as it remains to this day."

"I am glad to be home, finally, my good Count," Ewelina said. "My life has only been filled with misery since I left here."

"Yes, *Pani* Ewelina," the Count replied, all the while not taking his eyes off Magdalena, "this one causes us all both great pain. She and her son Marek together have cost me a fortune."

"It doesn't appear you are in need of it," Magdalena said. "The *folwark,* the mine, these buildings - all stolen from the Duke. Just as you stole my own title and holdings as well."

"The thing about great riches," Count Von Arndt replied, "is that they only make you hunger for more. *'Avarice has so seized mankind that their wealth seems rather to possess them than they to possess their wealth,'* Pliny the Younger said in the beginning of the second century. I am afraid it has only become more true as the succeeding centuries have passed."

"Well, I have nothing left for you to take from me except my dignity," Magdalena said.

"Oh, as you did mine?" the Count responded sharply. "Disgracing me out of favor with the Viennese Court? I am sure you recall, we were to be wed, until your damned son deserted to the French. But here, today, you will make it up to me. Indeed, you are the key to great riches after all."

The Count looked upon her with a sinister leer. She did not understand his reference to "great riches."

"As I said, Count," Magdalena repeated herself, "I have nothing left for you to steal."

"Except your son, Marek," Von Arndt countered. "He will be made aware of your predicament shortly, if he has not already. He will surely attempt to rescue you with others under his command. When he does, my guards will cut them down, every last one. Then, I will *'be shocked to discover'* they are soldiers of the French Empire and protest this incursion to Vienna. With a bit of luck, the incident might even incite another Austrian war with France. In any case, I will obtain my revenge on both you and your son, receive a financial settlement from Vienna and possibly ignite a war to drive up the price of my salt. In any case, you and your Marek will learn not to bring disgrace on someone of my repute."

"So you dangle me as a mere piece of bait," Magdalena accused. "Just as you did Marek's false injuries to lure me here!"

"Yes, exactly," he said as he walked over in the darkening dusk and lit the oil lamp on the small table, "but don't be angry at yourself, for it was a masterfully conceived plan. If you must address your anger at anyone, I could not have made this all happen without the help of your sister-in-law, Ewelina."

"I have no anger for her," Magdalena said, "as only someone as pathetic as yourself would prey on those already suffering from so great a loss as her own."

"As you shall soon suffer yourself," the Count said. "For I will make sure that when I do destroy your son, you will be able to watch his death from this very window. Until he arrives, you will both be kept here. Marek will be made aware of your imprisonment as soon as he reaches Warsaw. I suspect it to be another two days before we can expect your son and his allies here to attempt to rescue you. In the meanwhile food will be brought in for you both. Oh, and my apologies, Magdalena, but I had the inkwells removed from the room. I do recall just how resourceful you proved to be with them."

With that, the Count departed the guest house. Ewelina and Magdalena were locked together in that second-story room where they would spend the next several days under the crushing weight of an icy silence.

Marek Zaczek, having led the escort of the beautiful young Countess Marie Walewska to Warsaw, assisted the woman from the coach in which she had traveled.

"*Dziękuję,* my brave Colonel Zaczek," the Countess thanked him for escorting her.

"A mere Lieutenant Colonel, Madame," he corrected her.

"Nonetheless," she said, as her things were removed from the coach by the footmen, "the Emperor speaks so highly of you. He told me you were among those who saved him from being captured, or worse killed, at Eylau." With this she leaned forward and kissed him tenderly on the cheek. "For this especially I owe you my thanks."

"*Nie ma za co! (It is nothing!)*" he replied, blushing lightly from the softness of her lips as they found the rough skin of his face. "I was just one of many doing just as we are trained to do."

"Well, I am happy to thank you for your service to the Emperor. He is quite proud of you. You know who else is so proud of you? My governess! Please come inside and let her see you."

"I am sorry, Madame Countess," Marek replied, "but I am afraid that I can not do that. My many regrets."

As he said this, the Countess reached out to grab the arm of a passing footman carrying one of her lighter bags. "Please go inside and ask Madame Zaczek to come outside. Tell her that her son Marek is here, and if she refuses, that I need her urgently."

"But Madame Countess," the house servant answered, "your governess has not been here for two days. She was unexpectedly called away to Sieniawa on urgent family business. But if this is Lieutenant Colonel Zaczek, we have a letter awaiting his arrival delivered yesterday by a courier. I will bring it forth."

"We have no family in Sieniawa," Marek stated, as a worried look crept over his face.

"Sieniawa is the location of the country home of Princess Izabela Czartoryska, is it not? Does she not provide for your mother? Does Magdalena not live in her Warsaw townhouse? Perhaps the Princess fell ill and was in dire need of her."

"Yes," Marek replied, "but that is perhaps the only reason my *matka* would ever return to Galicia? She fled from there to escape her past and traveled here to the safety of Warsaw with the Princess' assistance. That being said, I do not like this at all."

The footman arrived with an envelope and a silver letter opener on a matching tray, which he presented to Marek. Zaczek then picked up the message with great caution, ignoring the opener. He inspected the back of the envelope, and found its wax embossed with the imprint of a familiar but unwelcome seal. His concern deepened.

"I can tell by the look on your face that you recognize that seal," the Countess said. "Whose is it?"

"The Austrian Count Maximilian Von Arndt," Marek replied. "It can only mean trouble, I am sure."

"*Proszę,* go ahead, Marek, open it," the Countess said, in haste forgetting herself and calling him by his Christian name as his mother had so often in discussing her son. "I must know what this message says."

Marek looked at her, and could see her concern was sincere. His mother always spoke so very highly of the Countess.

Marek decided he would share the contents with her. He removed the dress uniform glove from his right hand and slipped his forefinger under its flap. The seal cracked open like the fresh fissures in his heart. He unfolded the note and read it to himself.

"Well," Countess Marie asked, "what does it say?"

"It is not good," Zaczek replied.

"Tell me. I demand that you tell me!" The Countess' words were unusually tense, but Marek attributed their directness to the great fear that edged their utterance.

"It says that my *matka* is at the Count's *folwark* under the care of Doctor Olszewski. She was injured traveling in a coach accident nearby. It says I must come immediately, alone."

"Oh, how terrible!"

"Madame Countess," Marek explained, "something does not make sense here. Your footman says the house was told that my *matka* traveled to Sieniawa. This note says she is in Wieliczka. It is neither close to nor on the way to Sieniawa. The only common attribute is that both are in Galicia. I must believe that she was lured into that Austrian province by some ill news, and once over the border, she was taken forcibly by the Count to his *folwark.*"

"If that is true," the Countess Marie said in her still agitated voice, "then this is an outrage. Why would Magdalena need a doctor's care in that case?"

"I doubt that she does," Marek replied. "The Count wants to take his revenge against me, and his claim against her health is merely my incentive to come at once."

"Why would the Count want you, Marek?"

Marek was unsure of how much of his story, or for that matter her own, his mother had shared with the Countess. He was inclined not to answer her, but realized that the woman had a great concern for his mother. The Countess had a tender heart, that was clear to him, so he decided that she deserved an explanation.

"My *matka* told me long ago," Marek finally began, "that the Count blamed all his losses on my defecting to the French years ago. He lost a fortune, my *matka's* fortune to be truthful, that he, until then, planned to take from her by marriage. It appears my defecting to the French put an end to his scheme. For this, he has long desired revenge on both she and I. It is likely that the Count fears that I might hesitate to attempt to rescue her due to our estrangement, or because any incident that might risk the Emperor's hard-won peace would be met with severe punishment. So he lures me with false news, I am sure, that she is injured."

"Or perhaps he knows that despite the Peace of Tilsit," the Countess thought through the situation aloud, "you would still come to your mother's aid in any case. He is simply using the ruse of her injuries to get you to act rashly and in haste instead of carefully planning out what needs to be done. He hopes your emotions will overtake your caution. I am greatly troubled, Marek. He very well may plan to kill you both."

"Yes," Marek said, "that all certainly could be very true, but it changes nothing."

"So then what will you do?" she asked.

"I will take my time, as you suggest, and gather what I need to be successful, and on my own schedule. Only then will I go to take my *matka* back from him," Marek said, "the Emperor's peace be damned."

"I can help you. What do you need?" The Countess asked, anxious to assist him in any way she possibly could.

"You are still on excellent terms with Grand Marshal of the Palace, General Duroc? I will give you a list of men that I need, most are already here in Warsaw, but one is from Toruń. Have him dismiss them so they can meet me in the Kraków *Rynek* at six in the evening in two days time. Also, I will need a small amount of funds to cover my expenses. Can you loan those to me?"

"I can certainly get you both with no difficulty," Marie responded, "but I would rather you allow me to raise this to the Emperor for his intercession. Or at least allow me to have General Duroc provide you an overpowering number of men."

"Absolutely not, Madame," Marek objected. "I cannot have the Emperor or General Duroc associated with what I must do."

"Which is what exactly?" Marie asked.

Marek ignored her and took a pencil from his uniform pocket to scribble down the names of five soldiers on the back of the note from the Count.

"Here," he said simply, "these are the men I require. Make sure they are told this is a volunteer tasking only. They can say no to my request."

"And what happens when one or more do so?" she asked.

"They won't," he said confidently. "They'll know I am in dire need or I would not ask this of them. Not a man will deny me his services, I am sure."

"You will rescue Magdalena?"

"Of course. What else can I do? This is an affront to all civility, and I plan to assure that nothing like this will ever happen again to my family, or that of anyone else."

"Precisely how will you do that?" Marie asked.

"I will kill Count Von Arndt," Marek said resolutely.

Marek departed immediately upon leaving the Countess and rode to see Maya. He dismounted and ran up the steps of the outside staircase and into the Warsaw townhome much to Maya's shock. She rushed to him and threw herself into his arms without thinking, so overjoyed was she to see him alive and in good health.

"My Marek," she cried out, her face pressed against the uniform covering his powerful chest. "I am so relieved to see you. I was told you were dying! You do not look injured to me at all. Where is *Matka* Magdalena?"

"I was prepared to ask you the very same question," he said, taking her by the shoulders and peeling her from his frame.

"She did not return from Sieniawa with you?"

"I was never there," he answered. "Why would I be?"

"The message from Princess Czartoryska said you were there and badly wounded. Clinging to life, in fact."

"Ah, so that is how Count Von Arndt got Magdalena to enter Galicia. He has her back at his Wieliczka *folwark* and demands I go to them. Where is Tolo? I need him."

"What are you going to do?"

"I need Tolo! Where is he? Do not hesitate to ask me questions. And I need my civilian clothes. Are they still here?"

"Yes, you have britches and your blue *zupan* upstairs, but what do you need all this for?"

"I leave in an hour. Tell Tolo to meet me in Kraków at the *Rynek* outside the Cloth Hall in two days at six in the evening."

"Not unless you tell me what you intend to do…"

"You remember the night I came to take you from the *folwark* to elope? I plan to use that same route of escape with Magdalena. Only this time, I will take some of my fellow Polish Lancers with me. This time, I will most certainly be successful. Now, I need my clothes…"

Chapter 19: The Rescue From Wieliczka

July 30th, 1807

The clip-clop fall of the single mare's hooves on the long gravel road rang out in the still night air as loud as pistol shots. Marek Zaczek felt a twinge of nostalgia rip through him as he tread this path for the first time since being shipped off by Duke Sdanowicz to the Austrian military over a decade earlier. The sound bounced off the trees lining the path and echoed a series of eerie reverberations that haunted the night.

Marek arrived at the doors of the manor house, where a lone house servant awaited. He did not recognize the old man who took the reigns of his horse, and wondered if he was an Austrian manservant long in the Count's employ. Marek told the man in German to keep the animal at the ready, for he would be leaving very soon. The servant replied in Polish, "Very good, sir."

Marek was shown inside by a second servant, and led into the Count's den, where the man himself was seated at a desk going over papers. Across from him sat Doctor Olszewski. Both men looked much older than he had recalled, and somehow this made him feel as though the years had worn them down mercilessly. He wondered if they had the opposite surprise of himself, as he was but a young man, not much more than a boy, when they had last laid eyes on him. He decided it did not matter, for they would see just how much of a man he had become soon enough.

"Ah, we have a visitor," the Count said to the doctor, as he rose in recognition of Marek's presence. "I see you received my letter, although truly I thought you'd have been here by last night."

"Hello, Marek," the doctor said as he also rose. "It has been a very long time. I have been looking forward to your arrival."

Marek was annoyed at the mock civility shown him by the two men. He pulled a pistol from the band around his waist.

"You both know why I am here. I have come to collect my *matka*. Where is she? And Magdalena had best not be in need of any of his caring, I warn you." The last comment, directed at the Count, was accompanied by a head nod to Doctor Olszewski.

"Marek, Marek!" the Count called out, showing no excitement over the weapon being pointed at them. "I assure you that you are in no need that pistol. Of course, your mother is uninjured. Neither is your Aunt Ewelina, by the way. I apologize for the inaccuracy of the note, but it was merely an inducement to have you come visit the land on which you were raised."

"That message was nothing more than an outright lie to be conveniently turned over to the authorities when all this affair is properly investigated," Marek said. "Nothing more."

"And why exactly would any of this need to be investigated," asked the Count, "properly or otherwise?"

"Because I intend to take Magdalena and leave. As for my Aunt Ewelina, I have no use for her. I assume she was part of your plan to lure my *matka* here. Now, take me to them and don't force me to kill you both before I leave for Warsaw."

"Well," the Count said nonchalantly, "that sounds very threatening indeed. I had better take you to them. And yes, your aunt did assist the good doctor and I. She is welcome to stay on the *folwark* for as long as she likes, even perhaps for the rest of her life. After all, it is where her family all rests, is it not? Her husband, her twin sons. Your cousins, remember. She and I both share one thing, Marek. You have ruined both of our lives."

"Yes," Marek replied. "It appears your days have been so terribly ruinous." He motioned to the opulence of the manor house surrounding him.

"All frozen in time since you defected to the French, my young man. By now, I should have been so much wealthier, living in a much less modest home in Vienna, not in this God forsaken backwater. No, Marek, your traitorous actions sentenced me to this place, but tonight I will even the tally."

"Save me your words and just take me to my *matka,*" Marek demanded, motioning with the pistol barrel.

"But of course. You have the weapon after all," replied the Count. "Come this way." Taking a lamp from across the room, he led Marek to the back door of the manor house. Doctor Olszewski stayed behind in the den. The two men exited the manor house and followed the short stone walk up to the guest house. Marek noted the wagon of hay that sat pushed against the structure, oddly out of place. He thought he noticed the hard glint of the lamp's firelight off steel hidden beneath its straggly load. In a window directly above the wagon, flickered the light of another lamp, outlining a feminine form peering out at them. Marek instantly recognized the backlit shape as being that of his mother.

Marek, with his pistol still drawn and pointed at the Count's back followed him into the guest house and up the steps of the staircase. At the landing above them, the Count reached into his pocket and produced a small skeleton key. He inserted it into the keyhole of the chamber door, turned it, and both slowly walked in.

"Marek!" Magdalena ran to embrace him. She threw herself at him, having no regard for the pistol which he instinctively lowered. The Count made no attempt to flee; he merely stood and watched the reunion of mother and child as if everything were playing out exactly as he had foreseen. The manner with which he carried himself told Marek that the Count had a surprise turn of events at the ready.

Marek was comforted knowing that, as it turned out, so also did he.

"*Matka*," Marek said as he kissed her. "Are you harmed in any way?"

"No, my dear," she said, pressing her face against his, "I am fine. I am perfectly fine," she whispered as she squeezed him tightly, "but you should not have come. This is all a trap."

"Of course it is," he whispered in reply, "but I have a few surprises for the Count of my own. We will be leaving very soon."

"Are you satisfied?" The Count said, holding out his hands palms upward. "I suggest we go back to my den and finish our conversation, Marek. Then we can return, and you and Magdalena can leave together."

"Why do I need to discuss anything further with you at all? I will take her now and we will depart."

"I fear not, Marek," the Count said. "For no sooner had you approached up the gravel path, it was sealed off by my *folwark* guards. You see, your only hope to exit this place is by coming with me."

"I should just shoot you, here and now," Marek replied.

"That would be very satisfying for you, I am sure," the Count said, "but you would both be dead in minutes thereafter. No, Marek, we have much to talk about. I have a very generous offer for you. You surrender yourself to me, and I will release Magdalena tonight. She will be free to return to Warsaw."

"Don't listen to him, Marek," his mother called out. "If you surrender to him, he shall only kill us both."

Marek looked at the woman who was to blame for all this. His Aunt Ewelina stood behind Magdalena, partially obscured in by her shadow. "I hope you are quite proud of your treachery. You should fear the wrath of God for what you have done. He will not forgive you for your deceit!"

"I have already felt the wrath of God," his aunt replied, "the day I helped deliver you, the sinful birth that you were. I would have done best to have thrown your infant self directly onto the fire."

Marek could only shake his head at her vile, bitter comment before he turned back to Magdalena.

"I will be back shortly, *Matka,*" he said, kissing the tender skin of her forehead. He gently pushed her away and pointed the weapon again at the Count. "I will take that key. I don't want your men slipping in here after we leave."

"That is a very reasonable request." The Count showed no concern and handed the skeleton key to him.

The two men left the chamber, and Marek locked the door behind them. Magdalena and Ewelina remained inside, watching from the window as the two emerged from the building onto the stone pathway below. As they did, the two women saw the pair being cut off by two of the Count's guards from the front, with another pair coming up from behind. Marek would be forced to turn over his weapon. Magdalena feared her son would be killed then and there as she watched from the window, just as the Count had intended all along.

On the stone path below, Marek saw the shape of the two guards who moved forward to block their return to the manor house. Then he turned to look over his shoulder when he noticed the pair that came up from behind. He had assumed all along that some move along this path would likely be the Count's play. He glanced at the upstairs window to see his mother's backlit silhouette moving away from her place at the window.

"I'll take that weapon, Marek," Von Arndt said, as a knowing smile creased his face. "Please don't try any heroics, as the rest of my men guard the gravel path, the only way out of the *folwark*."

"You forget I was raised here," Marek replied. "There are an infinite number of ways to escape this *folwark*, including being forced into conscription to the military of the country that stole our Polish lands. No, tell your guards to back away, or I will shoot."

"You have only a single shot in that pistol," Von Arndt said, "and there are five of us in total. These four men are all excellent swordsmen. You'll never live to escape, nor would your mother."

"Then I suppose I will just have to save this shot for you, Count," Marek said, raising the gun to the Count's head.

"Kill me and you'll ruin your Emperor's peace and start a war between Austria and France. Even if you somehow could escape, how would your Emperor respond to that assault on his newfound peace with all of Continental Europe?"

Marek looked beyond the two guardsmen in front of him, both on foot, to see the outline of a rider on horseback in the shadows just beyond the edge of the guest house.

Magdalena had watched everything below. She could see Marek was outnumbered, not only by the four guards on foot around him on the path, but she also saw horsemen with sabres hiding in the darkness at both ends of the building.

"Now you will taste what it is to have your family stripped away from you!" Ewelina said. Her face showed no emotion but only a sinister resolve. She was about to get her just revenge, one she had waited for so long.

Magdalena knew she must do something quickly. She looked below at the wagon of hay, and a thought entered her mind. Magdalena looked at the flickering oil lamp in her hand.

"What are you going to do?" Ewelina asked.

"I will create a diversion for Marek," Magdalena replied, "by setting that wagon of hay below ablaze. Perhaps it will distract all the guards and allow my son to escape."

"No, it is the only light we have," Ewelina said. "We will be in complete darkness. Besides, that window does not open, I have already tried it many times."

"Neither is of any concern to me," Magdalena said, swinging the oil lamp. Its full reservoir of liquid sloshed within it as she did so. "I will throw this lamp through the glass, and it will land in the wagon below. The resulting fire will create a great distraction in which Marek can run off into the darkness of the night. I cannot stay here and do nothing but watch my son die."

"No. You must do exactly that, and feel my pain," Ewelina said. "Watch, and suffer. Suffer for the rest of your life, just as you and your son have damned me to do. Now, give me that lamp."

With this, Magdalena drew back the lamp to hurl it as she took a few steps closer to the window. But as she did, Ewelina tried to stop her, to disrupt her from throwing away their only source of light. Magdalena fought with her, and soon she was able to free the lamp and hurl it at the glass pane. However, as she did, Ewelina hit Magdalena's arm as she released the lamp, but it was too late. The lamp had already left her grasp, but due to Ewelina's intrusion, its path was altered. It shattered not through the glass of the window as Magdalena intended, but rather struck its heavily lacquered wooden frame.

The lamp shattered into many pieces upon impact, causing the full reservoir of oil to ignite and then explode in all directions. The window frame and curtains were instantly set ablaze.

Magdalena felt the slap of flying liquid on the right side of her face, followed by an intense biting pain and the smell of her own burning flesh. The skin around her eye was aflame, its brightness blinding her sight. She brought the skirt of her dress up to her face to smother its open flames, and as she did she heard a blood-curdling scream come from Ewelina. When she let the folds of her dress fall away, she looked up to find her sister-in-law positioned between herself and the blazing window frame. Both it and Ewelina were entirely engulfed in flames.

Her clothes completely on fire, Ewelina wrenched and howled before the wickedly dancing flames of the window frame. Its panes of glass, still intact, reflected the distorted, surrealistic details of the hellish scene. The fiery victim screamed in gut-wrenching agony, just before, when in an act of sheer panicked desperation, she threw herself through the glass in a final attempt to escape the cruel intensity of the flames by smothering them out in the wagon of hay below.

The smashing sound of the lamp on the upstairs window broke the tension of the men on the path. Everyone looked up to see the flames instantly engulf that elevated window box. Marek knew his mother was in great peril, and that he must act immediately.

Before he could, he was shocked to see a flaming body come crashing through the glass of the upper story's window. This was a sight he had seen several times before on the battlefield. There was nothing more sickening than the pathetic flailing of a human being whose skin was ignited. Their arms and legs were frantic with horrid motion, clutching for any chance of escape, any relief from the insufferable pain, of which there was none.

Marek watched helplessly as the writhing, burning body fell the dozen or so feet into the wagon of hay. He feared this was the pathetic end of his mother's life. His stomach dropped from within him as he looked up, only to follow the descent of the flame-engulfed form. In the last second, he saw another ghoulish silhouette peering down at them. Marek could make out a look of compassion and concern upon its own heinously burned and disfigured face, and knew at once that he glanced upon what had moments before been the lovely countenance of his mother.

Marek then watched as the falling figure thudded into the hay wagon. As soon as Ewelina's flaming body landed in it, compressing its wispy load, several thick metallic spikes hidden beneath the hay impaled her burning body. One of which pierced the back of her skull and mercifully ended his aunt's last torment of agony. The wagon was quickly transformed into a funeral pyre, filling the air with the thick acrid smell of roasted flesh.

Of all else that Marek might have expected to hear in that devilish moment, the nervous chuckle that came forth was the last thing he could stand. Marek's head snapped to face one of the two guards in front of him, who had burst into half-arrested laughter watching Ewelina throw herself down only to have the sharp, thick tines of hidden metal puncture her smoking corpse. Marek looked up at the man's snarling grin and instantly realized that this must be the guard who had set the trap, most likely at the Count's direction. Marek, repulsed by his snickering, before he even fully realized what he was doing, raised the pistol and shot the self-amused scoundrel in the face from only a few feet away.

Upstairs, the intense heat drove Magdalena back away from the window. The inrush of the fresh night air stoked the flames, which had spread to the ceiling. Soon, the entire room would be engulfed, and Magdalena realized her fate would be the same as Ewelina's. Her burned face was already searing with pain. She retreated from the window, looking one last time down at Marek.

The Count and his remaining three guards surrounded him. They moved toward her son just as four other men on horseback closed in. The plan had always been for the pistol shot to be the signal to engage. After firing its shot that dropped the first guard, Marek fell to the ground and rolled under the flaming wagon. He stayed down and out of the way as the four horsemen moved in.

The first to make his pass was Edziu, his sabre slashing at one of the guards with a vicious lethality that was only matched by the rider's anger. Then, from the other direction, rode in Mieczysław with his sword swinging an arc of deadly accuracy. Two of the three remaining guards were dead in the seconds of that initial pass, but the confusion of the moment allowed the two remaining men to run off. Antoni and Rydek both moved to cut down the last guard, who was armed. The Count made his escape into the manor house. Then Klęczeć Sałeh appeared on foot, leading two horses, one being Marek's mount taken from the front of the manor house.

Marek crawled out from under the flaming wagon. He knew he must act quickly to save his mother from the flames above. As he ran into the foyer of the guest house, he heard the groaning of the timber above him as it twisted in the flames.

Marek ran up the stairs and produced the skeleton key to the bedchamber. As he worked it into the lock, smoke poured out from under the door. He hoped he was not too late. He opened the door only to be faced by veils of thickening fumes. Then he heard the choking gasps of his mother. He rushed into the room, and as the fire surrounded them, he searched frantically for his *matka*.

Marek found her, crouched down, her arms wrapped around the thick leg of a table that the lamp had been placed upon. He could see she was in great shock. As he reached down to gather her into his arms, he again smelled the sickening burning of human flesh. He saw her face, the entire right side burned away, leaving an ashen char that made her look ghoulishly deformed.

Marek picked his mother up and told her that everything would be alright,

"How did you escape those horsemen?" she asked.

"Those are my riders, *Matka*," he said. "Each man volunteered to risk his life to save yours. We must not let them down. Now, come, we must go quickly."

Marek lifted her and carried her down the steps. He placed her on his horse before climbing up in the saddle behind her. It was then that Antoni came alongside and looked upon the burned face of Marek's mother. He looked away and whispered to his leader that the gravel road exit was blocked by guards on horseback."

"I anticipated that," Marek said, taking his sabre and scabbard from the saddle." That is why we brought along my trusted river man, Tolo. Come, follow me. He awaits us."

Marek then raced his mount across the night-darkened lands of the *folwark,* leading Antoni, his brother Edziu, Mieczysław, Rydek, and Klęczeć Sałeh. The terrain was exactly as he remembered it from his boyhood adventures. He made for the location across the fields to where the dense woods of the *folwark* touched the shores of the Vistula River. This was the site of the three-fingered rock, the same spot where long ago he had attempted to escape in eloping with Maya. He failed then, but this time he knew that Tolo would be waiting to raft them all to safety.

The five riders each dismounted and tied off their horses at the edge of the dense forest to navigate the rest of the way on foot. Marek had Antoni carry Magdalena so he could lead the way. The others followed, and all soon noticed they were making their way toward a shimmering light which illuminated the darkness. As they closed in on it, Marek was able to make out the source of the brightness, and his heart sank in his mouth. Standing on the three-fingered rock was Tolo. Beyond, only a foot or two away in the Vistula was the raft intended to carry them to safety. It was floating free, raging with fire, consuming their only route of escape.

"What happened?" Marek said to his oldest friend.

"They were waiting for me…" Tolo replied.

"Who?"

"Them!" Tolo replied. From out of the shadows of the woods came eight men, all strongly framed and brandishing drawn swords. As they moved in, they cut off the group's escape by land.

Marek looked at them and took measure of their chances. Under any normal situation, six Polish light horsemen, not counting Tolo, who was unarmed, might be an even match for eight *folwark* guards, but as Marek thought through their odds, another nine men came up behind them. These were the guards who had blocked the gravel road entrance, accompanied by Count Von Arndt himself. Now, the numbers were quite seriously stacked against them. Seventeen to six, even after they had already killed off four of their comrades in front of the guest house.

The seven of them prepared to fight: Marek was framed on either side by Tolo, Rydek. Antoni (who carried Magdalena), Edziu, Mieczysław and Sałeh. They stood around the three-fingered rock, fanned out in a semicircle with their backs to the river. Marek knew exactly how precarious their position was. Their options were simple - fight to the last man, or be prepared to drown in the river trying to escape.

Magdalena was laid down by Antoni onto the flat rock just behind her son. She was by then deeply in shock from the severe burns to her face and no longer seemed to sense what went on around her. It was just as well, perhaps she might not be aware of the butchery that awaited each of them.

The guards spread out against them in an even larger semi-circle, with an advantage of well over two to one, all with swords readied for the final attack. Marek called out the command, *"Sabres!"* and each of his men drew his blade, save the unarmed Tolo. It was then that the Count stepped forward to address Marek.

"Do you know how many times Doctor Olszewski told me the story of your trying to elope with the Duke's daughter. I knew you would flee to this same spot, but I didn't suppose you would even have the same boatman who had failed you in the past." He pointed to Tolo. "That proved to be a most unlucky choice."

"It has not been proven so yet," Marek replied bravely. "Bring on your guards. We will fight until the last of us falls. But be warned that even if we all fall here on this spot, your treachery will not stand."

"Marek," the Count continued, "prepare yourself and your men to die. Guards, show these men no mercy, no quarter. I suggest you slice them up into bits so small they are readily digestible by the carp in the river."

"You men, know that we will all fight to the death," Marek called out to the guards directly. "It is likely that you will overpower us, but each of you should know we are trained killers. We will take at least half of you with us. This is your last chance to walk away."

The guards laughed, but nervously, for they knew that some number of them might be lost in the melee that was about to ensue.

"So be it," Marek yelled out, "then let us proceed, you bastards!"

"Marek," Count Von Arndt said, "from my understanding, you are the only true bastard among all of us. Yes, the good Doctor shared that with me also. You know, for being such a decorated military man, I find it humorous, beyond all compare, that you are in precisely the same situation as the Russians at the Battle of Friedland - with your backs to the river."

Both sides held their sabres high, ready for the slaughter to begin. The Count waited a brief second before he backed up from between the two armed lines, laughing as he said, "I thought that was the greatest mistake any band of soldiers could ever make!"

"No," a very heavily accented voice called out from the darkness behind them all. "That is only the second worst place a warrior can find himself. The first is between the pincers of two well-trained and armed lines of their enemy."

Someone among the guards yelled out the word that created fear in the hearts of all, *"Cossacks!"*

Then a single command in the Ukrainian was given, and the swishing of a dozen arrows loosed in unison flew from seemingly nowhere amongst the trees, striking only the *folwark* guards. A second salvo quickly followed. Not a single guard escaped their flight. Marek and his companions then stepped forward to finish off each and every one of the arrow-riddled guards with the swift slashing, slicing strikes of their sabres.

As the melee ensued, Bohun and his dozen Cossacks came out into the open, but did not join in the slaughter. They were all attired in their traditional, colorful Asiatic uniforms, complete with their high, dark fur hats. Bohun walked up to Marek, saying only, "once again, you look ridiculous in that *Zupan.*"

Count Von Arndt ran off into the darkness of the forest, and a pair of Cossacks pursued him. He was quickly chased down by the *Zaporozhians.*

Bohun barked out so commands in the tongue of *the Sich,* then said, "I told them to hold him for you to finish off, Marek."

Marek walked over to the Count. He held to Von Arndt's neck the blade of his sabre, which still dripped with the blood of several of the slaughtered guards.

"I will enjoy taking your life most." Marek boasted.

Antoni then became the voice of reason. "Killing this man will only be an excuse for another war. Let the son of a bitch live. He is one building and a contingent of guards poorer. Let him live to lick his wounds. We will walk away with your *matka,* victorious."

Marek looked upon his chief of staff, almost disbelieving the words that he had heard from him.

"Antoni, how can you say this? You carried my *matka in your arms*. Victorious? You saw what was done to her face!"

Antoni's brother, Edziu, weighed in, "Antoni, let him kill the Austrian already. That way, we will not be needed to come back and do it later ourselves."

Marek peered down at the Count, still held to the ground by the two Cossacks. Sweat-drenched terror had replaced the smug self-assured look upon his face from only a few minutes before.

"Marek," Antoni reasoned with him, "remember that the burning of your mother's face was her own doing. This man did not set those flames."

"No, he surely did," argued Marek, peering down into the Count's terrified eyes, "by setting this all in play. He was prepared to have her try and escape into that wagon of hay in which he had so sickly hidden those spikes, as my Aunt Ewelina found out."

"And most mercifully so," Klęczeć Sałeh called out, joining Antoni in his mercy. "Do not kill the man. We are done here. Leave him to suffer his losses."

"Mieczysław?" asked Marek.

"Do as you see fit," the master swordsman said. "I cannot blame you for wanting to take his life. Yet, I would like to think that under similar circumstances, I, myself, might not."

"Rydek?"

"The man deserves to die for what he has done, it is true," his friend answered. "But while it would feel like justice, I fear it might be viewed as murder by some, and France and Austria could be driven to war once more by his death."

Mare pondered their words, but the injuries his mother would bear for the rest of her life, assuming she even survived this tragedy, countered against their advice.

Time stood still, but not Marek's raging fury. He fought to control it. Finally, he reached a compromise of sorts.

"All right, I will listen to you all, but the Count shall not leave these woods unmarked," Marek said. As he did, he moved the tip of his sabre down from the Count's neck. With great dexterity, he flicked his wrist and cut away the buttons of his shirt. "Bohun, have your Cossacks pull open his *chemise.*"

Bohun called out some words in Ukrainian, and the men obeyed. The men presented the Count's bare chest to Marek.

With this being done, Marek scrawled the script letters

into the skin of the man's chest, producing a great scream of pain from the Count as he did so. Blood gushed out across his chest.

"I suggest, Count," he said, "that you have Doctor Olszewski attend to that wound. He will recognize it as the same mark I once made on my two cousins that you now have buried in your cemetery. But remember, on them these were my initials. Here on your chest, I have inscribed my *matka's* mark. You once told her you wanted her hand in marriage, so it is only fitting you will carry for the rest of your natural life her initials on the skin above your heart."

With this, Marek made a hand gesture, and the two Cossacks released the Count. As he writhed in pain on the forest floor, Marek walked back to Bohun.

"I am most thankful for your showing up when you did…" he said.

"We have been trailing you ever since you left Kraków," Bohun said.

"…but how did you even know about this raid at all?"

"Maya, of course," he said. "I stopped by to collect Orest," referring to his infant son, "from her after the peace was declared and my Cossack band was released from its service to the Russians. Seeing my son's face again made me reflect on your having allowed me to live, to escape from that forest at Friedland. So when Maya explained what was going on, I gathered my men for one last bit of excitement. They were all happy to come along. But I tell you here and now, my friend, our slates are wiped clean. I am no longer indebted to you, nor you to me. The next time we engage in war on opposite sides, I will not hesitate to kill you."

"Let us hope that day never dawns," Marek said. "Now, I thank you one last time, then I must get my mother to Kraków to get attention for her burns."

Chapter 20: Epilogue

The Peace of Tilsit marked what would later be called the summit of Napoleon's power and influence. It created the Grand Duchy of Warsaw, Napoleon's half-measure in reconstituting the Polish state, which failed to satisfy anyone wholly. It was carved from the Prussian lands in the east, while the western Prussian provinces were consumed to constitute Westphalia.. In total, Prussia lost half of its land mass in the punishing peace settlement.

Alternatively, in taking no lands at all from Tsar Alexander, Napoleon gained his Russia as an ally under the Tilsit accord, achieving an even greater aspiration. His Berlin Decree from the end of 1806 established the blockade of all English merchants from doing trade with Continental Europe. There was only one problem with the so-called *"Continental System"* - it did not work.

After the Battle of Trafalgar in late 1805, Britain had near complete command of the seas. This included a well-developed network of ships smuggling British goods onto the continent. In addition, some countries refused to participate in the blockade, most notably Portugal, and this would lead Napoleon into what would become the pathway to his final downfall via the chronic Peninsular War, which would start the following year in 1808. This conflict would introduce Britain's land forces onto the continent under Field Marshal Arthur Wellesley, to be remembered more ubiquitously by history as the Duke of Wellington.

The Poles would press on living under the Grand Duchy of Warsaw for five years until after their support of Napoleon's disastrous invasion of Russia in 1812. The Tsar's outright refusal, by then, to adhere to *"The Continental System"* played a major role in initiating that ruinous invasion.

It is most interesting that in 1807, Napoleon had absolutely no interest in invading Russia. He knew his troops, so long away from home, were beleaguered and had been pressed near to their limits. As we will see in future volumes, five years later, the Emperor would not show that same restraint, and would press his troops well beyond what any soldier could ever be asked to endure. During that campaign of 1812, a great price would be paid by the Poles, for they would make up more of the *Grande Armée* than any other nationality, other than the French.

The Polish Lancers would remain loyal to Napoleon to the end, fighting in the Peninsula War in Spain with sabres, taking up the beloved lance once more against the Austrians at Wagram, joining Napoleon to invade Russia on that ill-fated campaign of 1812, and even join the Emperor in exile at Elbe. Of course, they would go on to serve ever so remarkably in the 100 days return to France, and distinguish themselves in their bravery at Waterloo.

All that bound the Poles in their loyalty, not to France, *per se,* but to the Emperor Napoleon personally, had been set in place at the conclusion of the War of the Fourth Coalition with the Peace at Tilsit. And, for now, this is where our story will end.

The End of

"The Life of Marek Zaczek

Volume 3: The Precipice of Peace"

Figure 26: Emperor Napoleon Reviews the Polish Light Horse Regiment (Lancers) in Exile at Elba in 1814 (Painting by Polish Artist Jan Chełmiński)

Author's Notes

I wish to sincerely say **"Dziękuję bardzo"** or "thank you very much" for your time dedicated to reading this third volume of this historical saga, **"The Life of Marek Zaczek."** It covers a much more limited period of time, as opposed to Volumes 1 & 2, and thus is a more compact story. But the seven months from January 1st to July 30th in 1807 proved to be the critical element cementing the relationship between Napoleon and the Polish people.

In this timeframe, both parties experienced considerable success: Napoleon had his victory over the Russians and the peace was made at Tilsit; the Poles achieved the re-emergence, in part, of their heritage and culture in *"The Grand Duchy of Warsaw."* The ties binding both far into the future included the establishment of the regiment of Polish Lancers (even though they were forced to forgo that weapon temporarily, which is historically accurate) and the kindling of the flame of a great love that would burn for years to come between the Emperor and his "Polish Wife," Countess Marie Walewska.

Napoleon would become smitten with Marie; She was so much more than a mere mistress. He would later bring her to Paris, and then to Vienna. She would be the only of his loves to visit him during his exile at Elbe. She would bear him a son, proving the Emperor's virility. If Napoleon had a recurring complaint, it was that she always dressed so modestly in tones of gray and black. Napoleon wished for more elegant and lively attire from her while in his company, to which she is reported as having replied:

"A Polish woman must wear mourning for her country. When that is restored to life by you, I will wear nothing but rose-color.[40]*"*

---

[40] *"Sex Life of an Emperor: The Many Loves of Napoleon Bonaparte,"* by Frederic Masson, 2009, Fireship Press LLC, Tucson, Arizona.

Not to infer that the Poles were *"Janny-Come-Lately"* supporters of Napoleon, after all, as the Polish General Dąbrowski had supported the Emperor long before his coronation. But after the Emperor came to Warsaw, the Poles would remain steadfast supporters of Napoleon until his bitter end. They would go on to fight on his behalf in most of his major battles that will be highlighted in future volumes of this series. They would engage once more against the Austrians; follow Napoleon on his ill-advised forays into Spain and later Russia; and die in the streets of Leipzig as the Empire collapsed. They even joined Napoleon on his first exile to Elba, on his hundred days march afterward, and the Poles even fought heroically on his behalf at Waterloo.

If you are wondering about the various use of the Cossacks by the Russians, what I describe throughout this work is historically accurate. While the Cossack Bohun is fictional, it is true that Cossacks intercepted Napoleon's commands prior to the Battle of Eylau. In fact, it caused Marshal Bernadotte to arrive two days late and miss the battle in its entirety. Also, Napoleon's ploy of sending false orders intended to be captured by Cossacks prior to the Battle of Heilsberg is also accurate.

This title is subtitled, *"The Precipice of Peace."* Napoleon reaches his zenith, but like all conquests it can be a very short-lived accomplishment. This story details exactly how that peace was achieved. Volume 4 of *"The Life of Marek Zaczek"* will describe how it all began to slip away. I hope you will join me for it. One thing is certain, it is bound to be a very exciting ride.

Appendices:

Appendix A: Source Materials/ Suggested Historical Reading

Appendix B: List of Image Attributions

Appendix C: Countries of the Coalitions Within this Volume:

Appendix D: Countries of the Coalitions Beyond this Volume:

Appendix E: Pronunciation Guide for Polish Terms:

Appendix F: Pronunciation Guides for Polish Character Names:

1) ***"The Campaigns of Napoleon,"*** David Chandler, Folio Society Edition (2002) in Three Volumes of the Orion Publishing/Scribner (1966) Original (One Volume).

2) ***"The History of Napoleon Bonaparte,"*** R. H. Horne, George Routledge and Sons, London,1879.

3) ***"The Life of Napoleon,"*** William Milligan Sloane, The Century Company, New York, 1896, 4 Volumes.

4) ***"The Life of Napoleon Buonaparte,"*** J.G. Lockhart, Bickers and Son, Leicester Square, London 1889.

5) ***"Napoleon's Polish Gamble"*,** Christopher Summerville, Pen & Sword Military Publishing, 2005.

6) ***"Memoirs of a Polish Lancer: The Pamietniki of Dzeydery Chłapowski"*,** Emperor's Press, 1992.

7) ***"Poles and Saxons of the Napoleonic Wars"*,** George Nafzinger et al., Emperor's Press, 1991.

8) ***"Talleyrand"*,** Duff Cooper, 1932, Folio Society Edition.

9) ***"The Diary of Marie Walewska,"*** Transcribed from Walewski Family Archives, March 2006 by Alexandre Christian Walewski.

10) ***"Marie Walewska (Les Maîtresses de Napoléon)"*** by Frédéric Masson, E. Guillium, 1897.

11) ***"Napoleon's Elite Cavalry, Cavalry of the Imperial Guard, 1804-1815, Paintings of Lucien Rousselot,"*** Text by Edward Ryan, Published by Greenhill Books (London) and Stackpole Books (Pennsylvania), 1999.

12) ***"The General Correspondence of Napoleon Bonaparte,"*** www. Napoleonica.org, Les Archives, Foundation Napoléon.

13) ***"Napoleon's Polish Lancers of the Imperial Guard"*** by Ronald Pawly, Illustrated by Patrice Courcelle, 2007, Osprey Publishing Ltd.

14) ***"Polish Soldiers During The Napoleonic Wars,"*** Soldiershop Publishing, May 2018, Edited by Luca Stefano Cristini.

15) ***"Sex Life of an Emperor: The Many Loves of Napoleon Bonaparte,"*** Frederic Masson, 2009, Fireship Press LLC, Tucson Arizona.

Front Cover Layout:

Original Marek Zaczek Portrait by Madeline Trawinski (Used with Permission)
Age Progressed by David Trawinski

Composited Public Domain Images

    a) *"Combat d'Eylau le 7 février 1807: attaque du cimetière,"*
       by Jean-Antoine-Siméon Fort, Public Domain.

    b) *"Napoléon après la bataille d'Eylau, le 9 février 1807,"*
       by Antoine-Jean Gros, 1808, Public Domain.

    c) *"Equestrian Portrait of Alexander I (1777–1825),"* by Franz Krüger, 1837,
       Public Domain.

    d) *"Porträt of Louise of Mecklenburg-Strelitz, Queen of Prussia,"*
       by Josef Grassi, 1802, Public Domain.

    e) *"Portrait de la comtesse Walewska,"* by Édouard Dubufe, 1859,
       Public Domain

Dedication Image: *"Panorama of Assumption Church,"* Kyiv, Ukraine
       Adobe Stock Image License #87441065 by esvetleishaya,

Back Cover Images:

    a) *"A Polish Lancer of the First Regiment of Napoleonic Polish Lancers
       (circa 1807),"* by Édouard Detaille, Public Domain.

    b) *"Zaporozhian Cossack,"* by Konstantin Makovsky, 1884, Public Domain

    c) *"Photograph of Königsberg between 1894 and 1900,"* Wikimedia,
       Photographer Unknown, Public Domain
       (Horizontally inverted and cropped)

    d) *"Kolumna Zygmunta III Wazy 2020.jpg"* by Adrian Grycuk, 8 May 2020,
       Used under Creative Commons Attribution Share Alike Poland License

    e) *"Dobre Miasto"* Photograph by Jerzy Strzelecki, 2007,
       Used under Creative Commons Attribution 3.0 Unported License

Interior Images:

Figure 1: *"Map of Europe 1804 - 1806,"* Created by David Trawinski, 2023
       using licensed Adobe Stock Image #110535933 by Peter Hermes Furian

Figure 2: *"Map of Napoleon's Prussian Campaign of 1806 -1807,"*
       Created by David Trawinski, Copyright 2023

Figure 3: "Painting of Napoleon Bonaparte," by Jacques-Louis David, 1813,
       Public Domain

Figure 4: *"Charles Maurice de Talleyrand Périgord (1754–1838), Prince de Bénévent"*
       by François Gérard, 1808, Public Domain

Figure 5: *"A Polish Lancer of the First Regiment of Napoleonic Polish Lancers
       (circa 1807),"* by Édouard Detaille, Public Domain.

Figure 6 : Map, *"Russian Winter Attack Across East Prussia,"*
       by David Trawinski © 2025

Figure 7: *"Leonty Leontievich Bennigsen (1745 - 1826), Russian Count
       and Cavalry general,"* by George Dawe, 1820, Public Domain

Figure 8: *"Portrait de la comtesse Walewska,"* by Édouard Dubufe, 1859, Public Domain

Figure 9: Map, *"Napoleon's Russian Trap,"* by David Trawinski © 2025

Figure 10: *"Zaporozhian Cossack,"* by Konstantin Makovsky, 1884, Public Domain.

Figure 11: *"Combat d'Eylau le 7 février 1807: attaque du cimetière,"*
by Jean-Antoine-Siméon Fort, Public Domain

Figure 12: *"Bataille d'Eylau, 8 février 1807, l'armée russe repoussée
par la charge de la cavalerie et de la Gar,"*
by Jean-Antoine-Siméon Fort, Public Domain

Figure 13: *"Maréchal Ney à Eylau,"* by Richard Caton Woodville, 1913, Public Domain

Figure 14: *"Napoléon après la bataille d'Eylau, le 9 février 1807,"*
by Antoine-Jean Gros, 1808, Public Domain

Figure 15: *"Schloss Finckenstein,"* Wikipedia Commons, Public Domain.

Figure 16:: "Equestrian portrait of Wincenty Krasiński," by Théodore Géricault, c. 1814
with overlay of "Le général Wincenty Krasiński,
colonel du 1er régiment de lanciers polonais
de la Garde impériale et comte d'Opinagora."
Both Works Public Domain.

Figure 17: *"Prince Józef Poniatowski, Commander in Chief of the Army of the
Duchy of Warsaw,"* by Josef Grassi, Circa 1810, Public Domain

Figure 18: *"Entry of Napoleon and the French Army in Gdańsk 1807,"*
by Adolphe Roehn, 19th Century, Public Domain

Figure 19: Map, *"Battles Along the Alle River," by David Trawinski © 2025*

Figure 20: *"Maréchal Michel Ney, duc d'Elchingen, prince de la Moskova,"*
by François Gérard, c. 1805, Public Domain.

Figure 21: Map, "Prelude to the Battle of Friedland," by David Trawinski © 2025

Figure 22: *"Vive l'Empereur! (Charge of the 4th Hussars at the battle of Friedland,
14 June 1807),"* by Édouard Detaille, 1891, Public Domain

Figure 23: Map, "The Battle of Friedland," by David Trawinski © 2025
With Force Projection overlay from map: Battle of Friedland
United States Military Academy, West Point, Public Domain

Figure 24: "The Battle of Friedland, June 14,1807," by Horace Vernet, 1839,
Public Domain.

Figure 25: *"Porträt of Louise of Mecklenburg-Strelitz, Queen of Prussia,"*
by Josef Grassi, 1802, Public Domain.

Figure 26: *"Elba Squadron of the 1st Light Horse Regiment Polish Lancers
of the Imperial Guard"* by Jan Chełmiński, c. 1925, Public Domain.

Interior Chapter Heading Graphics and Dividers produced by David Trawinski
by modifying the following Licensed Adobe Stock Image:

Napoleonic "N" image using AdobeImage # 392927897 by Alex Birch

Appendix C: Countries of the Coalitions Within this Volume:

(Simplified)

Revolutionary War of the First Coalition (1793 –1797)
Coalition: Great Britain, Spain, Holland, Holy Roman Empire (led by Austria),
   Prussia, and Piedmont-Sardinia
Result: French Victory
   France annexes the Austrian Netherlands
   France annexes the Left Bank of the Rhine
   France establishes satellite republics in Northern Italy
   The Thousand-Year Ducal Empire of Venice is dissolved by Napoleon
Ended by: Several treaties including the Treaty of Paris (1797) with Piedmont-Sardinia

Revolutionary War of the Second Coalition (1798 -1802)
Coalition: Great Britain, Spain, Holland, Holy Roman Empire (led by Austria),
   Russia, Naples, Ottoman Empire and Portugal
Result: French Victory, Egypt occupied, French fleet destroyed
   at Battle of the Nile (1 October 1798), Italian territories regained by France
Ended by: Treaty of Amiens with British on March 25, 1802 and
   Treaties of Paris with Russia on 8 October 1801
    and Ottoman Empire on 25 June 1802

Napoleonic War of the Third Coalition (1805 - 1806)
Coalition: Great Britain, Holy Roman Empire (led by Austria),
   Russia, Naples, Sicily and Sweden
Result: French Empire Victory,
   The Thousand-Year Holy Roman Empire dissolved,
   Confederacy of the Rhine created,
   Combined Spanish/French fleet lost in Battle of Trafalgar
   Austrian and Russian armies defeated at Austerlitz
Ended by Treaty of Pressburg with Holy Roman Empire under Francis II
   Signed on 26 December 1805

Napoleonic War of the Fourth Coalition (1806 - 1807) (Continued in Marek Zaczek 3)
Coalition: Great Britain, Prussia, Russia, Saxony, Sweden and Sicily
Result: French Empire Victory
   Defeat of Russia and Prussian at Battle of Friedland
   Ended by Treaty of Tilsit (7 July 1807) with Russian Tsar Alexander I
    and Prussian King Frederick Wilhelm III
    Prussia lost half of its Territory with
     Napoleon's creation of The Duchy of Warsaw
   Creation of the Continental System of embargo against British trade.

The Peninsula Wars (1807 - 1814)

Coalition: United Kingdom, Portugal, Spain\

Result: War of Attrition which eventually gave the British army a foothold on the Continent and which brought them eventually into Southern France

Napoleonic War of the Fifth Coalition (1809)

Coalition: United Kingdom, Austria, Sardinia and Sicily

Result: French Empire Victory after Battle of Wagram

Ended by Treaty of Schönbrunn

The Russian Campaign (1812)

Combatant: Russia

Result: After Russia Lures Napoleon into a desolated Moscow, the French Empire Withdrawals, Resulting in the defeat and obliteration of the invading *Grande Armée*

Napoleonic War of the Six Coalition (1813 - 1814)

Coalition: United Kingdom, Russia, Prussia, Austria, Spain, Sweden and Portugal
Result: French Empire Defeated at Leipzig in the "Battle of the Nations"
Ended by Abdication of Napoleon, Exiled to Elba

Napoleonic War of the Seventh Coalition (1815)

Coalition: United Kingdom, Russia, Prussia, Austria, Sweden and German States
Result: French Empire Defeated at Waterloo
Ended by: Abdication of Napoleon, Final Exile to Saint Helena

Term	**_Meaning_**	**_Pronunciation_**
Pan	Sir	*Pahn*
Pani	Madame	*PAHN nee*
Proszę	Please	PRAH she(m)
Dziękuję	Thank you	Jeh(m) KOO ye(m)
Babcia	*Grandmother*	*BAHPT tsha*
Ciocia or Ciotka	Aunt	CHUTCHee/CHUTCHka
Do widzenia	Goodbye (informal)	Doh Vee ZEHN ya
Do zobaczenia	See you later	Doh Zoh ba CHEN ya
Dobronoc	Goodnight	Doh BRAHN oots
Dzień *dobry*	Hello/Good day	Jane DOH bree
Dobrze	Good or Well	DUB zha
Dupa	Ass (Derriere)	*DOO pah*
Dupek!	You Ass (Insult)	DOO Pek
Dziękuję bardzo	Thank you very much	Jeh(m) KOO ye(m) BAHD zo
Nie ma za co	It is nothing! (Dismissive)	Nee ma zats so
Folwark	A Nobleman's Estate	FOL vark
Ówniarz	Sh**head, Punk	GOOV nash
Matka	Mother	MAHTka
Moja	My	MOI ya
Proszę bardzo	You are welcome	PRAH she(m) BAHD zo
Tata	Daddy	TA ta
Stare Miasto	Old Town	STAHRee Me AS to
Szlachta	Nobleman	Szlahta
Witamy	Welcome	VeeTAM mee
Zona	Wife	ZONE ah
Zupan	A noble's garment	ZUH pohn

Fictional Polish Character Names   Pronunciation

Marek Zaczek	*MAH rek ZAH check*
Maya	*MAI ya*
Magdalena	*Mahg da LEENE ya*
Jacek	*YAHT sek*
Ewelina	*Eva LEEN a*
Rydek	*RYE dek*
Władek	*VWA dek*
Czesław	*CHES wav*
Bronisław	*Brohn NIS wav*
Bartek	*BAHR tek*
Andrzej	*AHND jay*

Historical Polish Character Names   Pronunciation

Izabela Czartoryska   **Izabela Char tor REE ska**
  Princess, renown art collector, creator of first Polish Museum

Adam Jerzy Czartoryski   **Adam Yerzy Char tor REE skee**
  Son of Princess Izabela, Patriot, Foreign Minister to Tsar Alexander I

General Jan Henryk Dąbrowski   **Yan HAHN reek Dom BRUV skee**
  Patriot, Creator of Polish Legions under Napoleon in Italy

General Tadeusz Kościuszko   **TAH deush   Kohsh SHOOZ ko**
  Patriot, American War of Independence Hero, Leader of 1794 Uprising

Lancer Dezydery Chłapowski   **Dez eye DER ee   Hwa PUV skee**
  Patriot, Famous Polish Lancer in Service to Napoleon

Prince Jozef Poniatowski   **YO zef   Pahn yee a TUV Skee**
  Patriot, Nephew of last king of Poland, Ally to Napoleon

Marie Walewska   **Marie   Wa LEV ska**
  *Young Wife of Count Athanasius Colonna-Walewski forced by her
  countrymen to become a mistress to Napoleon Bonaparte,
  with whom she then fell madly in love.*

Novels by David Trawinski

The Chopin Trilogy *(WWII/ Cold War Espionage)*
    The Willow's Bend (2016)
    Chasing the Winter's Wind (2017)
    War of the Nocturne's Widow (2018)

The Deekie and Clay Series (Co-authored with Marie Trawinski)
    Ever Blooms the Rose (2019)   *Civil War/Reconstruction*
    Guns of the Yellow Rose (2022)   *Reconstruction/Western*
    Petals of the Christmas Rose (2025) *1875 Murder Mystery*

The Cord McCullough Westerns (Co-authored with Marie Trawinski)
    The Untouched (2024)   *1874 Texas Frontier Thriller*

The Churchill Series *(World War I and II / Espionage)*
    The Twins of Narvik Part I (2021)
    The Twins of Narvik Part II (2021)

The Life of Marek Zaczek Series
    (Partitions of Poland/Napoleonic Wars)
    Volume I: Under the Wings of Eagles (2020)
    Volume 2: Embers of Love and War (2023)
    Volume 3: The Precipice of Peace   (2025)

All Proudly Published by